Marx
Hardy
Joyce
Austen
Defoe
Abbott
Montaigne
Machiavelli
Emerson
Cooper
Chesterton
Hugo
Grimm
Melville
Eliot
Carroll
Christie
Haggard
Molière
Stoker
Maupassant
Byron
Schiller
Wilde
Engels
Garnett
Fitzgerald
Hawthorne
Smith
Kafka
Goethe
Einstein
Dostoyevsky
Hall
Cotton
Kipling
Doyle
Willis
Baum
Henry
Nietzsche
Leslie
Dumas
Flaubert
Turgenev
Balzac
Stockton
Vatsyayana
Crane
Burroughs
Verne
Curtis
Tocqueville
Vinci
Homer
Widger
Tolstoy
Whitman
Gogol
Busch
Darwin
Thoreau
Twain
Potter
Scott
Plato
Harte
Zola
Lawrence
Dickens
Kant
Freud
Jowett
Stevenson
Burton
Hesse
Andersen
London
Descartes
Cervantes
Poe
Aristotle
Wells
Voltaire
Burton
Hale
James
Hastings
Cooke
Bunner
Shakespeare
Richter
Chambers
Irving
Doré
da
Chekhov
Shaw
Wodehouse
Benedict
Dante
Pushkin
Alcott
Swift
Newton

 **tredition®**

tredition was established in 2006 by Sandra Latusseck and Soenke Schulz. Based in Hamburg, Germany, tredition offers publishing solutions to authors and publishing houses, combined with world-wide distribution of printed and digital book content. tredition is uniquely positioned to enable authors and publishing houses to create books on their own terms and without conventional manu-facturing risks.

For more information please visit: www.tredition.com

TREDITION CLASSICS

This book is part of the TREDITION CLASSICS series. The creators of this series are united by passion for literature and driven by the intention of making all public domain books available in printed format again - worldwide. Most TREDITION CLASSICS titles have been out of print and off the bookstore shelves for decades. At tredi-tion we believe that a great book never goes out of style and that its value is eternal. Several mostly non-profit literature projects pro-vide content to tredition. To support their good work, tredition donates a portion of the proceeds from each sold copy. As a reader of a TREDITION CLASSICS book, you support our mission to save many of the amazing works of world literature from oblivion. See all available books at www.tredition.com.

Project Gutenberg

The content for this book has been graciously provided by Project Gutenberg. Project Gutenberg is a non-profit organization founded by Michael Hart in 1971 at the University of Illinois. The mission of Project Gutenberg is simple: To encourage the creation and distribu-tion of eBooks. Project Gutenberg is the first and largest collection of public domain eBooks.

Kitty Canary

Kate Langley Bosher

Imprint

This book is part of TREDITION CLASSICS

Author: Kate Langley Bosher
Cover design: Buchgut, Berlin – Germany

Publisher: tredition GmbH, Hamburg - Germany
ISBN: 978-3-8424-8284-5

www.tredition.com
www.tredition.de

[Frontispiece: Kitty Canary.]

CONTENTS

KITTY CANARY

CHAPTER I

I am in love. It is the most scrumptious thing I have ever been in. Perfectly magnificent! Every time I think of it I feel as if I were going down an elevator forty floors and my heart flippity-flops so my teeth mortify me. He used to be engaged to Elizabeth Hamilton Carter, the niece of the lady at whose house I am boarding this summer, but he did something he ought not to have done, or he didn't do something he ought to have done, and they had a fuss. No one seems to know the cause of it, but it was probably from her wanting him to be blind to everything on earth but her, and a man isn't going to be blind when he wants to see, and then she got *hurt*. I'd rather live in a house with a cackling hen or a grunting pig than the sort of person who is always getting hurt. But she's very pretty. Pink-and-white pretty, with uplifting eyes and a little mouth that shuts itself when mad and says nothing, and oozes more disagreeableness than if it talked. He still thinks there isn't another girl in town who can touch her in looks. I don't suppose a man ever gets over a real case of pink-and-white. It's the kind that makes a tender memory if it isn't the best sort to live with, and men like to have a memory to sigh over in secret. Her rejected one may sigh in secret, but in public he does not seem to be suffering. He isn't suffering. We like each other very much.

The reason I am glad I am in love is that I am sixteen and I was getting afraid I wasn't ever going to fall in love. Three or four times I have thought I was in it, but I wasn't, and I was beginning to be sure I was the sort of person who doesn't fall. And, besides, it is good for Billy, who, because he is twenty, thinks he is old enough to have some things settled which there is no need to settle too soon. Settled things are not exciting. I love excitement and not knowing what a day may bring forth. Billy doesn't. He wants his ducks to be always in a row.

Ever since he fished me out of the water-barrel sunk in Grandmother Hatley's garden, when I was four and he eight, he has seemed to think I belonged to him; and, though he doesn't imagine I know it and never mentions it, he is always around when I am in danger or trouble, to get me out. I suppose saving my life three or four times makes him feel I can't take care of myself and therefore he must take care of me, but that's a mistake. I have never had a horse to run away with me but once. Billy did tell me not to ride her, and when she ran and would have pitched me over her head and down a gully he caught her in the nick of time and caught me, too, but that's the only time a thing of that sort ever happened. He was real nice about it and never said anything concerning having told me so and didn't make remarks of the sort which other people rub in, but the next day the horse was sent away. That's the thing which makes me fighting furious with Billy sometimes. He doesn't say things. He does them. I wasn't afraid of that horse and was going to keep on riding her, but the next day there was no Lady-Bird to ride. The reason he sent her away was I wouldn't promise not to ride her. Our summer homes are on adjoining places and Horson, their stableman, a nice, drinky old person, lets me take out anything I want, anything of Billy's, and, knowing he couldn't trust Horson any more than me, he lent Lady-Bird to a man miles and miles away and I never saw her again until she was a tame old thing I did not want to ride. Billy behaves as if I were a child!

And then the very next winter I fell through the ice and he had to jump in and get me out. He told me not to go to a certain part of the lake. He had been all over it and tried it before I got my skates on, but I forgot and went. A boy was with me, a skunky little rat, who, when he saw the ice was cracking, tried to pull me back, and then he let go my hand and flop I went in and flop came Billy behind me while the little Fur Coat stood off and bawled for help and said afterward he didn't know how to swim. Having on heavy clothes, I went down quick and was hard to get up, and I would be an angel this minute if Billy hadn't been there. But Billy is always there, which is what makes this summer so queer. He isn't here.

On account of servants and things his mother didn't want to open their country place this year, and my mother didn't want to open hers, so two houses are closed. That means a scatteration for both families and is why I am here and Billy in Europe; and if he is having as good a time as I am he isn't grunting at the change. He didn't want to go to Europe. His father made him. His mother and two sisters needed a man along and, as Mr. Sloane couldn't go, Billy had to, and he was a great big silent growl when he went off. I wasn't. I wanted to come to Twickenham Town. We had passed through it once on our way to Florida and I have been crazy to come back ever since, and when I found Mother was going with Florine and Jessica to a splashy place I didn't want to go to I begged her to let me come here and board with Miss Susanna Mason and — glory be — she let me do it!

She is a sort of relation, Miss Susanna is, a farback one, but nothing is too far back to claim here, and everybody who is anybody is kin to one another, or kin to some one else's kin, which makes for sociableness, and I am having a perfectly grand time. In all the world there isn't another place like the one I am in this summer, and I am getting so familiar with a new kind of natural history that maybe some day I will be an authority on it. Ancestry is the chief asset of Twickenham Town, and though you speak with the tongues of men and of angels and have not ancestors it profiteth you nothing. That is, among the natives. Being an outsider, I have decided not to have ancestors, and I am going to see if the people won't take me in for myself. I have always believed a nice person was nice if there weren't any family shrubs and things, and a nasty one was nasty no matter how many coats of arms there were or how heirloomy their houses, so I have asked Miss Susanna please to excuse me if I don't call her cousin (we are seventh removed, I think she said), and also, unless she has to, I hope she won't tell any one my real name is Katherine Bird, but let everybody call me Kitty Canary, as everybody does at home. I think she thought it was very queer in me to say such things, but she smiled her precious, patient little smile, and, though she didn't promise, she evidently hasn't mentioned my sure-enough name, as no one here calls me by any other than the one Billy gave me when I wasn't much bigger than a baby. Just Kitty Canary will do for me.

CHAPTER II

The way I met Whythe (he's the one I'm almost perfectly certain I am in love with) was this. When I got to the station in Twickenham Town there was no one to meet me and take me to Rose Hill, which is Miss Susanna Mason's home and right far out, because the train was three hours late, and Uncle Henry, who drives the hack, and Mr. Briggs, who runs the automobile, had gone home. There wasn't even anybody to take my bag. I told Mother I had written Miss Susanna what train I would be on, and because she was so busy and Father away she trusted me to do things she had never trusted me to do before and didn't write herself, which is why I wasn't met. I did write the letter saying I was coming, but I forgot to mail it and found it in my bag when I got off the train and was looking for my trunk check. It was nearly eleven o'clock and nobody around but some train people who looked at me and said nothing. And then a young man who had got off the same train came up and took off his hat and asked if he could not do something for me, and I told him I hoped he could and I certainly would be obliged if he would do it as quick as possible, as it was getting later every minute and Mother would be terribly worried if she knew I hadn't been met.

"But where are you going?" he asked, and his eyes, which are his best-looking part, took me in from top to toe. When I told him I was a boarder for Miss Susanna Mason and would like to get to her house he said if I didn't mind a pretty good walk he would take me there with pleasure, and we started off. It was a perfectly gorgeous night. The stars were as thick as buttercups in spring, and the moon was magnificent and the air full of all sorts of old-fashioned fragrances, as if honeysuckle and mignonette and tea-roses and heliotrope were all mixed together; and as there didn't seem any real need of grieving because there was no one to meet me, I thought I might as well enjoy myself. I did. I could not help the train being late, and I didn't forget to mail my letter on purpose; and it was an accident, or coincidence, that a nice man should be on the same train I was, who lived in the place I was going to spend the summer in, and knew very well the house I wanted to get to. I didn't know he had been engaged to the niece of the house and hadn't been to the latter since the engagement was broken, and I must say as we walked along he didn't show any evidences of despair or things of that sort. He couldn't possibly have been naturaler or in better spirits, and he laughed from the time we left the station until we reached Rose Hill. Not knowing his history, I told him I had come to Twickenham Town because I thought it was the most delicious old place in America; the sweetest, slowest, self-satisfiedest, cocksuredest place on earth, and everybody in it was a character—that is, everybody over thirty. He said that let him out, as he was only twenty-five, but he wasn't sure some under twenty-five were not somewhat queer. They are, I have found out since.

He had left his bag at the station, but he had mine, which was right heavy, and seeing there was a good stretch of open road before we began to go up the hill on the top of which was Miss Susanna's home, I told him he had better sit down a minute and rest, and I got up on the worm fence and twisted my feet around the rail below, and looked at him before he knew what I was going to do. He coughed a little and looked at his watch and said it was rather late to be resting, as Miss Susanna might be going to bed, and that if I were not too tired he thought we had better go on; and I told him all right. And then, because I couldn't help it, I stood up on the top of the fence, balanced myself on it, and, opening my arms as if I were going to fly, sprang off and ran up the road ahead of him.

At the gate, which was open and through which I could see the rose-bordered path leading up to the white-pillared porch on which Miss Susanna and her niece were sitting, he shook hands with me and told me good night and said he hoped he would see me very often while I was in town, and I said I hoped he would. He put my bag down and told me to send one of the servants out for it, and went on down the road, which I thought was the queerest behavior I had ever seen in my life. I didn't know, of course, about embarrassments and broken engagements and things of that sort, and for a moment I stared at his back and then picked up my bag and went up to the porch with it. All the boarders had gone to bed and only Miss Susanna and her niece were on the porch, and as I came up the steps they got up and stared at me as if I had risen from the grave.

I hadn't thought there was anything wrong in my coming from the station at that time of night with a strange man until I saw the look on Miss Susanna's face when I told her I had done it. If I had been a brand snatched from the burning I could not have been folded to her bosom with more fervent thanksgiving or a more pained expression, and at first, still not understanding, I thought I had done right off the worst thing a person could do in Twickenham Town. I had walked a long way with a man who didn't have ancestors, perhaps. He had seemed all right to me, and I was awfully glad to have him, as otherwise I might have had to sit on my suitcase all night, for I certainly couldn't have come up with the man who swung a lantern, and he was the only other white one in sight. But I found out later it wasn't lack of ancestors that caused the sudden chill which fell over us when I mentioned Mr. Eppes's name. It was something else and—oh, my granny!—the look that pretty little pink-and-white person gave me when I said what I had done!

"Oh, my dear, my dear!" Miss Susanna put her arms around me as if I were a little ewe lamb that had been lost and was found, and in the moonlight her beautiful little wrinkles reddened as if she were responsible for a most grievous calamity, "To think of your being alone at a public station at this time of night! A young girl! And I had promised your mother to take such good care of you! I wouldn't have had such a thing occur for—"

"There hasn't anything occurred." I took off my hat and fanned hard and then followed Miss Susanna up-stairs into a big square room with a big tester bed in it, and if she hadn't been looking at me I would have climbed up in it and gone to sleep in my clothes, I was so tired; but she didn't leave me for some time. She couldn't get over my walking two miles with a strange man late at night, and presently I found out she hoped I wouldn't mention it to any one in the town, as in a little place—

"Oh, I know—" I sat down in another chair. "I know little places. I was in one once for a month. Every one in it knew everything every other person did and didn't do, and said and didn't say, and if they sneezed what for, and if they didn't sneeze why not, and it was more fun! But I won't tell if you don't want me to, and did my horse come? Father had her sent three days ago, and I hope you won't get uneasy if I am not always back on time—"

I stopped. She was putting my hat on the top shelf of the biggest old mahogany wardrobe that was ever built for human apparel, and

I knew right off that was one of the things the matter with pretty Miss Pink-and-White. She was spoiled to death. I picked up the coat I had dropped on the table and hung it up myself, and saw I would have to be the thing I hate most on earth—an Example. I must be careful or that precious old soul would be waiting on me just as she waits on everybody else, and I wasn't going to stand for it. And then she asked me if I were not hungry—said she knew I must be after such a long trip; and I told her I was starving, but I would not eat of a feast of the gods if it were right in front of me, as the only thing I wanted to do was to go to sleep, and for fear she might keep on inquiring about all my relations I kissed her good night and walked with her to the door and asked if she would mind if I did not come down to breakfast, and she said of course I must not come, that Elizabeth never came if she had been up late the night before, and that decided me. I was the first one down the next morning.

CHAPTER III

It was a perfectly grand feeling—-the feeling I had the next day and have had every day since I got here—that I was in a place where there wasn't a single member of my family to tell me not to do things I wanted to do or to do what I did not want to do; and usually as I dress in the morning I dance a new kind of highland fling which I made up for times when I feel particularly happy. Everybody is well and Mother and the girls are having a lovely time in a place where I would have had a stupid one, being neither grown up nor a kid, but an in-betweener—too young for some ages and not old enough for others; and here in Twickenham Town I am as free as air, and Father is coming to see me as often as he can. I can't let myself think much about Father or I would take the train straight home.

I had begged him to let me stay with him, but neither he nor Mother would agree. Just because I got the Grome medal at school they imagined I had studied too hard and needed a quiet, restful summer in the mountains; but I will never study too hard while on this little planet called the earth. I got the medal because Billy said

I'd never sit still long enough to study for it, and just to show him he very often does not know what he is talking about I made up my mind to get it.

The only thing I ever expect to work hard over is one book. I am going to write one book that the critics will call a Discovery. It is to be dull and dry and dreary, and therefore it will be thought deep and strong and big, and only a few people will know that it has been written. After that I am going to write books that sell, write what people want to read—things that make them forget for a few moments that at times this world is but a fleeting show and there is a good deal of rot in it. If I can I am going to make people laugh, though I don't think I can do much in that line. I see the funny side of things too quickly to ever be able to write them down, as that takes time; but I am certainly going to be cheerful, and I am not going to croak. I don't mean I am going to be smiling all the time. I am not. Perpetual smilers are more than human nature can stand. Nothing is ever wrong, everything is beautiful, their smiles seem to say, which isn't so. There is a lot of life that is wrong, and any day horrid, hurting things may pop up, but that doesn't mean you've got to sit down and make a bosom friend of dolefulness. Some of the things you can shake your fist at, and some turn your back on, and some you have to face; but no matter what happens you can buck up and begin again if you get knocked out or hit in the back. And that's what I hope I will have sense enough to do—get up and get a move on when things go wrong.

So far nothing has gone wrong in Twickenham. Everybody has been lovely to me, and all sorts of ages have been to see me and asked me to their homes, and if they know my name is not really and truly Kitty Canary they never say so or mention my family, which is very nice of them, for I am sure they must talk of who I am and where I came from, that being the first thing done here when a stranger arrives. The reason I think they haven't let me off among themselves is that one of Miss Susanna's boarders started to say something to me on the subject one day and I told her I was a very plain person, almost common, and she could tell any one she chose. She has never mentioned the subject since. Just Kitty Canary is all I am going to be this summer, and if anybody doesn't care for me as

Kitty Canary I don't care for them to care for me as Katherine Bird. So endeth that.

CHAPTER IV

I have seen him every day since I came — seen my station help in time of need — and I must say he bears bravely the dispensations of a female person. He is not dejected, and he still seems to find life worth living; and if he weeps in secret, he shows no sign in public of regrets; neither does he hide himself from the gaze of others, but is always to be seen when one goes down-town or to the homes of other people. I don't know how we happen to meet so often, but I never go out that he doesn't appear; and though he does not come in at Rose Hill, he comes to the gate, and I am afraid we stand at it a little longer than is necessary, especially if Elizabeth Hamilton Carter is sitting on the porch.

I wonder why Satan walks right into me every time I see that piece of pretty pink-and-whiteness! He has never taken possession of me in that way before; but something about her just starts him off, and before I know it I am doing what I wouldn't think of doing if she were not around. She is perfectly furious with me, and I must say her manners, if they are Southern, could be improved. At best she is not much of a talker, I have been told; but since I arrived her little mouth has been shut so tight that I wonder how she breathes; and if she has spoken a dozen words to me since the night I came, they were too between-the-teethy for me to hear. I didn't want her beau, and I wouldn't have dreamed of noticing him if I had known how she felt about him; but after she tried the freezing act on me I didn't tell Satan to get behind me, as I suppose I should have done. I just went along and took things as they came, and the first thing I knew I was in love myself, and from the words of his mouth concerning the meditations of his heart he seemingly has recovered from a former attack and is in for a new one. Maybe we were not as considerate of the rejecter as we might have been. Of course, I never knew for a long time why the engagement was broken. He didn't

tell me and no one else seemed to know, and when I found out—
But that was a long time after—when I found out.

His name is Whythe Rives Eppes. The only things I don't like
about him are his front teeth and his relations. He could get three
new teeth, but nothing in human power could rid him of his rela-
tives. There are four of them—Mother, Sister, Sister Edwina, and
Miss Lily Lou, and may God have mercy on the girl who marries
the male member of the family and goes into their home to live! He
is a perfectly grand sort to be in love with, and I am almost sure I
am in love or I wouldn't feel so thrilly when I see him coming. But
being in love is one thing and getting married is a very different
other, and there isn't a man person living I want to think of marrying yet. It's awfully interesting, too, to learn the different ways in
which love can be made. Twickenham Town may be slow about
many things, but in others it is so quick it takes your breath away.
Whythe became personal in conversation the fourth time I was with
him. It was at the Braxtons' party and conditions were favorable,
but, not expecting the turn that was taken, I was as excited as if I
had never heard remarks of a similar character before, and the first
thing I knew I had promised Whythe (he begged me to call him
Whythe) to go horseback-riding with him the next day. We went—I
on Skylark, who is the joy of my life, and he on a borrowed horse,
and we had a perfectly wonderful time. I don't think Whythe will
ever be much of a lawyer, but as a love-maker he hasn't an equal on
earth—that is, any I have ever heard.

As we rode down the main street of Twickenham everybody in
the town seemed on it. Princess Street is the only one called by a
name, though of course the others have names, and it is the place
where everybody meets everybody else and learns all the news; and
if anybody went to sleep that night without knowing that Whythe
and I had started on a ride at ten o'clock in the morning and didn't
get back until three it was because that person was too deaf to hear
and couldn't understand the movement of lips. I didn't know I was
doing anything I oughtn't, and if I did it I am not sorry. I had a
grand time. It was a gorgeous day and cool enough for me to wear
my brown-linen riding-habit and high boots, which, with a stock
collar and small sailor hat, made me look real nice, and the way the
people stared at me you would have thought they had never seen a

divided skirt before, and—oh, my granny!—the faces of the family (Whythe's family) as we passed their house! I smiled the politest and properest I knew and they bowed back, but in a way that made me laugh out loud when out of sight, and so did Whythe. And then we forgot them, forgot everything except it was awfully good to be alive.

CHAPTER V

The place we went to is very historic and interesting. Something happened there that was very important in American history, but I have forgotten what it was. Whythe told me, and as it doesn't matter, being over for such a long time, I haven't tried to remember. The sky was so wonderful and the river so winding and lovely and the air so delicious that yesterdays did not seem important and only to-day counted; and it was when we were sitting under a beautiful big water-oak that Whythe began to be terribly sentimental and say things that would have been more suitable for moonlight and shadows and things of that sort. But suitable or not, they were thrilly to hear, and I would have enjoyed hearing them if it hadn't been for an abominable feeling that Billy was right beside me hearing every word also, and with a look on his face as if he thought my new friend was the foolest yet. And presently when I couldn't stand it any longer (I mean stand Billy standing by) I got up suddenly and told Whythe it was time to go home.

I interrupted him in the midst of a beautiful sentence about my eyelashes, I think, or maybe it was something else, I don't remember; but anyhow when I jumped up he was very much surprised and wanted to know what was the matter. I couldn't tell him, but I was perfectly furious with Billy and the look on his face, which seemed to say what I'd heard him say often about fool-flum talk and feather-headed fellows and things of that sort. And I was so mad I rode so fast Whythe couldn't keep up with me or continue the conversation, but it has been continued since. That is the main theme, though the variations are always different. Whythe never seems to give out on variations.

Of course, all of Miss Susanna's boarders, which are only four besides myself, had something to say in general about the faithlessness of men and the flirtatiousness of girls, and how times had changed, and how you couldn't put your hand on any human being and feel you could trust him in these days, and how men were gobbled up before they had got their breath good after painful experiences, and dozens of other things on that order. And I had such a good time listening to them, though they didn't talk directly to me, that I'd forget at times and nearly screech out loud at the tones of voice in which they did me up, and then I would remember and try to look serious. But seriousness doesn't seem to fit my face—that is, seriousness over sillinesses—and it wouldn't stay on very long.

They thought it very indelicate in me to walk away with Elizabeth's sweetheart right before her eyes—that is, Mrs. General Games did, but Miss Araminta Armstrong, who is over fifty and by nature sentimental and sympathetic, said she supposed it was natural for youth to seek consolation, and Whythe, poor dear, had been so heartbroken at Elizabeth's behavior that he had been receptive to other influences of a pleasing nature, and she didn't think they ought to be so hard on him. And then, after more talk of that sort, she would sigh and look away at the mountains in the distance with a loved-and-lost look in her eyes, and Miss Bettie Simcoe would sit up and snort.

There's nothing sentimental or sympathetic about Miss Bettie. Neither is there anything in the earth below or the heavens above that she has not an opinion of her own about, but the one concerning which she has the most decided opinions is Man. She doesn't mince matters when she gets on him. Also, she is an authority on God. She can tell you exactly why He does things, and she quotes Him as if He were her most confidential friend, and the only thing which stumps her is why He made such a mess of what is considered His most important work. Mention a male person's name and up go her eyebrows and down come the corners of her lips and on the side goes her head, and nothing need be said for her opinion to be understood. She is positively triumphant over Whythe. She goes around with a "Didn't-I-tell-you-so?" expression oozing out of every feature of her face, and I think she tells Elizabeth she is fortunate to have discovered his fickleness so soon.

If Elizabeth thinks she is fortunate she has a queer way of showing it. She must cry a good deal at night, judging by her eyes in the morning, but the thing that's most the matter with her is madness. She can't take it in that Whythe is showing no signs of anxiousness to make up. She imagined, I suppose, when they had their fuss that it wouldn't last very long and that he would give in to whatever she wanted, and now that he isn't giving in she is so freezingly furious with me she barely speaks to me. She seems to think it is my fault and that my coming just when I did is the cause of the whole trouble. Though she never says anything directly to me, she makes remarks in my presence about the way men flirt in Twickenham Town and how dangerous it is, especially for young girls who have never had any experience in things of that sort and are deceived by it; and as she talks I just rock and rock if in a chair, and swing and swing if in a hammock, until she has said a good many nasty things, and then I get up and go up-stairs and bring down a box of candy Whythe has sent me and offer it to her with my most Christian forgiveness and most understanding smile, and, strange to say, she never takes a piece!

I don't mind her remarks. They're natural, and if she wasn't such a horrid little teapot I'd do anything I could to straighten out things; but until she behaves herself I won't. I am having a very interesting time being in love, and why should I stop just because a man she broke with isn't grieving, but is keeping himself in practice saying to me what he used to say to her? I am not going to stop until I think it is time and until both have learned a few things they ought to know before they get married. She is a vain, selfish, pretty piece of spoiledness, and I don't believe she knows what real loving means. She is the sort that wants what it hasn't got, and all the more if she thinks anybody else is apt to get it. If she had any sense she would get a beau *pro tem*. That is the best thing on earth to bring a man back to the straight and narrow, and Whythe is the kind of man who needs to be brought every now and then.

I gave her that for nothing one morning—I mean the suggestion in general, though of course not personal—and she looked at me as if trying to understand. And then something came in her face that must have been an idea in her brain (her brain is slow), for, two days afterward, she said she was going away. A week later she

went to see a rich aunt on her father's side who has a summer home
somewhere and corrals young men and compels them to come to it,
Miss Bettie Simcoe says. When she was gone a great weight seemed
lifted off everybody, and even the servants breathed better. As for
Miss Susanna, she was that lightened and relieved, though naturally not saying so, that she looked ten years younger, and I know now
it is true that some people in a house are like fruit-cake on a weak
stomach. They make life hard. I didn't say my prayers that night. I
just sang the Doxology three times as loud as I could and jumped
into bed. Praise is prayer.

CHAPTER VI

I have been here four weeks to-day. If there are any people in or
around Twickenham Town that I do not know, it is because they are
not knowable. I love people, and, being naturally sociable and not
very particular, I have had a perfectly grand time making acquaint-
ances with the high and the low and, the in-betweeners; and the sick
and well, and the dear and the queer, and the ancestrals and up-
comers, and the rich and the poor, and every other variety that
grows; and now I am as familiar with most of the family histories as
the oldest inhabitant. That's the nice part of living in a small place.
Something depends on you and you depend on all the rest of the
town, but at home you're lost in numbers and only a few know
you're living. Here everybody knows, also they know some things
that perhaps had better be unknown. As for talk, they are the best
talkers on earth, and there's no subject under the sun they won't talk
about. It's an inheritance, Father says, and has been handed down
from ages past, and, though they don't read very much, they can do
more with a little knowledge than most learned people with their
information, and they make anything they mention interesting from
the way they mention it. I love to hear them, and I've heard a good
deal.

Dear, precious Miss Susanna in the secrecy of my bedroom gave
me a little talk a few nights ago, and said she hoped I wouldn't
mind, but as I was young and inexperienced she thought it her duty

to tell me that I must be careful and not too informal, for certain people wouldn't understand; and that while the Holts were a very good, respectable family, still they were not— She stopped and coughed a little, and of course I understood, but I pretended I didn't, and told her they were perfectly healthy and I had had more fun with the Holt children than with any in town, but if she preferred they should not come to her house to see me I would just stop in theirs sometimes, as I would not like them to think I was afraid to go with them. I wasn't, for while I knew they were not historic, they were the most interesting children I'd ever seen, and it seemed pretty cruel that they were left out of things because they didn't have forefathers to hang on to, or money, which of course would speak for itself. And dear, angelic Miss Susanna, who is so worn out with boarders and their special kind of human-nature horridness at times that she's hardly got body enough to cover her soul, said I mustn't misunderstand her, but the Holts had never gone in the same circles as the other people I had met, and that customs, though unkind, were hard to overcome, and the oldest son—

I told her not to worry about the oldest son. He could go anywhere he wanted and with any one he wanted by the time he was through college, which his parents were working themselves to death to send him through, and it was very probable that several girls in town would be glad to add their grandfathers to his natural endowments before many years were over. But if she didn't care for me to accept his attentions, as Miss Araminta Armstrong called them, I could always have an engagement when he asked me to go anywhere. She looked so shocked and distressed that I told her I didn't approve of telling stories any more than she did, and for most sorts people ought to be branded, but I'd much rather tell one of that land than hurt a person's feelings. And it wouldn't be untrue to say I had an engagement, for I always had one to go everywhere and anywhere, even if I didn't keep it; and again she coughed and looked so pained that I took her in my arms and whirled around the room with her and told her not to worry about me, either. I wouldn't disgrace her by knowing the wrong people too well, but everybody had their peculiarities and one of mine was I was going to know anybody I wanted to. I always thought a lady could, and, besides, I liked any kind of person who was interesting, and the best born ones were often very stupid, which of course was the wrong thing to say. So I had to give her another whirl, and by the time she got her breath it was time to see about supper, and she has never referred to the subject since.

Miss Susanna is a darling little lady of the old school (whatever the old school was) and I love her, but I am of my time as she is of hers, and I don't see her way any more than she sees mine. She ought to wear hoop-skirts and brocaded silks and lace fichus and mits, and sit with her beautiful hands folded in her lap and her tiny little feet on a footstool, and instead she works from morning to night trying to help the good-for-nothingest servants that were ever hired by tired ladies, except Uncle Henson, and Aunt Mandy, the cook, who have been with her for years and years. She's worn out. That's what's the matter with Miss Susanna, and that selfish, lazy little piece of pinkness who is now away doesn't lift her hand to help her unless it is to make a cake occasionally. I don't know how to make cake and never expect to know, as very good kinds can be bought, but I can wash dishes. I do it every morning and she dries them, so limp Eliza can go up-stairs and clean up the bedrooms, and we have a beautiful time talking about what a change comes over human beings when they board. That is, I do the talking and she shakes her head at me, but it does her good, as it gives sound to things she can't say. Most of her time has to be spent in thinking what to put in people's stomachs and fixing it to be put; and, from the quantity that goes in, boarders must have much better appetites than people who keep house. They eat and yet are never full. There'll be no hope of heaven for me if I ever have to keep boarders. I'd sweep them out with a broom certainly once a week. That is, in my mind, if my hands didn't. But Miss Susanna will never sweep them out. The sanctuary in which I let out for her is the pantry, and all the things she won't say I say for her. Yesterday she laughed so she broke a cup.

CHAPTER VII

Father is coming to-morrow! I am so excited and happy that to-day, after I was safely out of Twickenham Town and there was no one to see me, I stood up on Skylark's back and held the bridle with one hand and waved the other in the air; and then I tried standing on one foot with the other one out, but I came near losing my balance and just did catch myself in time. Seeing a woman coming down the road in a buggy, with a baby in her lap, I got back in place before she saw what I was doing, but I needn't have done it, for it was just Mrs. Pettigrew, and she wouldn't have cared whether it was my head or my heels which were on the horse. She has eleven children and no husband to speak of, and what people do or don't do doesn't bother her. We stopped for a little talk and she told me about the roof leaking and the pig eating the baby's bonnet which Miss Katie Spain had given it last Christmas, and which was too small for its head, but was all it had; and that a kettle of soft soap had fallen off the stove and burned two toes of Sammy, the next to the youngest boy, and she would still be telling me things, but I told her Father was coming and I had to attend to something, and so she drove on.

I did have something to attend to, but I didn't attend right away, for the day was so wonderful I couldn't go in for a long time. The sunshine looked as if it had been washed and ironed, it was so clear and clean and crisp, and the wind in the trees said all sorts of lovely things to me, and I made up my mind that, no matter what happened in life, I was always going to remember that warm and sweet and sunny things are sure to come again, if at times they seem dead and buried, and that I would try not to see the cranks and queernesses of people as much as I was by nature inclined to do; and then I went right back to Miss Susanna's, and before I knew it I had said something I oughtn't, and to Mr. Willie Prince.

Every time I see Mr. Willie I thank God he is no relation of mine. He is the only man boarder in the house, which is another thing to be thankful for; but, though he is hard to stand, he is nearly sixty and a human being, and I ought to remember what I forget and yesterday I didn't remember. He was the only son of his mother and should have been a daughter, and in trying to make him one his maternal parent succeeded better than in anything else she ever attempted, Miss Bettie Simcoe says—and she ought to know, being his first cousin. His business is telling people what they don't want to hear; and, though he doesn't do any work, a hound dog couldn't run a rabbit down quicker than he can a piece of gossip, and when he isn't sitting on somebody's front porch fanning himself with a palm-leaf fan, from which he is never separated in summer, he is down at the drug-store hearing and being heard. He thinks he is handsome, and he is as proud of his pink cheeks as a goose of her gander, and I'm sure he puts something on them on cool days. If he could wear some blue ribbon on his sandy hair and have trousers and coats to match his fancy vests he would be perfectly happy. As a man he is a poor job, but as a Miss Nancy he is perfect, and when yesterday I came in from my ride he made me so mad that I popped out something I shouldn't have popped and before I knew I was going to do it.

He was sitting on the porch when I came up, fanning as hard as he could fan, and as I went by he stopped me. "I would advise you to be more careful when you go in wading at the creek, Miss Kitty," he said, "It isn't customary for young ladies in Twickenham Town to do such things and—"

"And where I came from it isn't customary for gentlemen to fol- low young ladies and see what they do," I said, and the minute the words were out I knew I shouldn't have said them, for his face got as red as a beet and he jumped up and walked into the house.

I don't know that he really followed Sallie Sclater, who's a visiting girl, and myself to see if we went wading, but we certainly went and had a good time doing it, though we had to dry our feet with my petticoat. But from the way his face went he must have made it convenient to walk in that direction and must have seen us, or he wouldn't have known anything about our going, as we were careful to look around before we took off our shoes and stockings. I can't endure him, but he is nearly sixty and I am only sixteen, and I shouldn't have spoken as I did; and possibly because I was so hap- py over Father's coming I told him last night that if I had said any- thing I shouldn't I hoped he would forget it and I, too, would forget what had been said. And that, of course, I knew gentlemen in

Twickenham Town never did anything gentlemen shouldn't, and that my quickness of speech was always getting ahead of me; and he looked so relieved that I am perfectly certain he followed us. But, anyhow, he was very pleasant last night and told a scream of a story about poor little Miss Lily Lou Eppes when she thought she had a beau. She had almost landed him when he got away. He's never been heard from since.

CHAPTER VIII

It's over — Father's visit is. He has been gone a week, and it will be a whole month before he can come again. He has to divide up between Mother and the girls and me, and he can only get away once in two weeks, because his partner is ill and business has something the matter with it and has to be watched, which is why he could stay only four days in Twickenham Town. I don't see why fathers have to work so hard, and why wives and daughters must have so many unnecessary things, and such big houses and so many new clothes and automobiles and parties and pleasures, which aren't real fun after you have them. But most women seem to want them, and keep on scrambling for what other people scramble for, and only a few have sense enough to see how foolish it all is and stop. Maybe they are wound up so tight they can't stop. I don't know. I only know I do not want to live the life a lot of women I know live, and I am not going to do it.

I wish Father could see it the way I do — about working so hard, I mean — and I think he might, for he says I am a chip off the block and he is the block, and in almost everything we feel alike; but there's Mother and the girls, who care for things I don't care for, and of course they must have them. He gives them everything they want, but he looked so awfully tired the day he came I could think of nothing else the night he left, which is why I cried so under the sheet, and then when the tears were out and I felt lighter I got up and wrote him a long letter and told him I loved him so it hurt, and that he was the best and dearest father on all this big, big earth, and if he would let me come and keep house for him I would fly back.

But he wouldn't let me come. He wrote me a letter, though, that I shall keep with my treasures, and I wish what he said was so. It isn't so. He just thinks it, but it does your heart good to know somebody cares an awful lot about you and no matter what you do is going to stand by. What he wrote me was this:

Dear little Nut-brown Maid all mine, of course you would come, but you mustn't. It is too hot and you need what you are getting, and nothing could help me here so much as to know of that wonderful color of yours and that you are so well and strong again. That you are getting health and happy memories for the winter of work and study ahead is the best tonic I can take, and every morning when I go to my desk I get out that little picture of you and, nobody being by, I kiss it and send you my love, and it is a breath of life-giving air to know you are mine. Since the first time I saw you – you were exactly one hour old and laughing even then – you have been the joy and delight of my heart, and I can't afford to run any risk with summer heat and the joy of my heart. I didn't deserve you, for I wanted a son so badly, and was fearfully disappointed that you were not a boy. You seemed to understand and did not get mad about it, and I've often wanted you to know that no son could mean to me now what my little harum-scarum daughter means. There has never been a day since you first looked into my eyes that I haven't thanked God for you, and the thing I am most afraid of in life is that you may get sick or not be strong, and that is why I am so glad for you to be in such a charming old place as Twickenham Town. You were wise, little daughter of mine, to choose so quaint and queer and dear a place in which to spend your summer, for there real things still count, and there is more time for the fine courtesies of life, and the hurry and rush of it, the push and scramble for place and power, is out of key with its quiet serenity and the poise that comes from a sense of values that by many of us is to-day forgotten. I am coming back as soon as I can, for I, too, want the refreshment and novelty of being where money is not talked and apologies never made for the absence of things that money gets. Miss Susanna Mason is a liberal education in herself and no "Course in Culture" could equal the advantage of being in her society. I have written her, of course, but tell her again of my sense of privilege, and my great pleasure, in being a guest in her home, and remember always you are in your father's heart. Always he is thinking of you.

Now wasn't that a nice letter to get from a father? I'm nothing to be thankful for; but, if he thinks I am, I am thankful for that, and it makes life a different thing to know somebody is thankful for you. And another thing I think would make life nicer, make working and living not so hard, is to tell people you like them and you believe they are trying to do their best, even if their best is powerful poor. Of course, all people don't try to do their best. Some are by nature and practice mean and horrid and ought to have facts handed out to them, but most people try to do right, and maybe they would try harder if they got a little encouragement now and then. Anyhow, I've often noticed it makes a person take fresh hold again for somebody to give them a lift in the way of a friendly word or so, and it doesn't cost much—kindness doesn't. I wonder why we don't have more of it.

The reason why Father liked Twickenham Town so much was that nobody talked business to him, and if anybody knew he was the head of Bird & Roller, bankers and brokers, they never mentioned it to him or talked shop at all, and for four days he forgot stocks and bonds and the ups and downs of the money-market and let go. And yet I am almost sure Mr. Willie Prince knows all about him—the business part, I mean—and that, of course, will mean everybody in Twickenham will know pretty soon. The reason I think he knows is that I went into the bank to get a check cashed the morning after Father got here, and I saw Mr. Willie sitting at a table in a corner of the bank with a copy of Bradstreet open before him and his eyes close to it. I made it convenient to walk up to the table and look down at the book, and I saw he was running his finger down the letter "B," and when he saw me he shut the book quick. I just smiled and passed on. But not talking business is only one of the reasons Father liked Twickenham Town so much. Another was because everybody was so nice to him. He had so many invitations to dinner and supper, and even breakfast, that he was on a dead go from morning until night, and he never ate so much in his life as he ate in those four days. It did him good, and he didn't look tired a bit when he left.

CHAPTER IX

The day Father got here was a beautiful day. The train was due at six-thirty in the morning, but it never hurries and has only been on time three times since it has been running, and Uncle Henson said there was no use getting to the station until seven o'clock, but I told him if he wasn't in front of the porch by six o'clock I'd send for Mr. Briggs and go down in his automobile, and there was no need to say anything more. Mention automobile to Uncle Henson and his back begins to go up just like a cat's. There are only a few automobiles in town, though a good many people have Fords, and several offered to lend me theirs, but not wanting to hurt Miss Susanna, who has been sending the same carriage to the station for over thirty years, I didn't accept their offers, but went down in the coach, as Uncle Henson calls it. Its top is still upholstered in a sun-shaped thing which was once yellow satin and now tattered and torn, and hardly anybody ever rides in it, but when a new boarder comes Miss Susanna always says, in that queenly way of hers, "You will take the carriage to the station, Henson," and Uncle Henson's old gray head bows as if at royal orders, and they do not know they are playing a part that belongs to the days that are no more. That is what Tennyson, I think, calls a time that will never be the same again.

Uncle Henson's coachman's coat, long and faded and once brass-buttoned, and a battered hat to match, are always put on to meet the train; and when he held the door open for Father to get in the old, ramshackle thing he did it in a way that could be sold for big money, if manner could be bought, and Father got inside with equal elegance. After he was in and Uncle Henson couldn't see him, he looked at me as if to ask if I thought it would stand, and I nodded back yes, and slipped my hand in his and hugged him again, I was so glorious glad to see him! He is such a splendid Father—my Father is, I am so sorry for girls who haven't one like mine, and not one of them has. He is the only one of his kind on earth.

Everybody was on the porch to meet us when we drove up, and Miss Susanna gave him such a gracious welcome, and was so sweet and stately and quaint and lovely in her white dotted Swiss muslin dress which Miss Araminta Armstrong says she has been wearing for six summers, and which has the dearest little darns in it, that

Father's face got real flushed, and once I really believe there were tears in his eyes. He might have been an ambassador at some court who was being received, for at no court in Europe could a lady bow as Mrs. General Gaines bows, and she gave her best to Father when he was presented. I don't like her, but she certainly is an old swell. And then Isham (he's Uncle Henson and Aunt Mandy's grandson, and totes water all day long from the well up into the house, when he isn't playing a Jew's-harp in the sun) came out and got Father's bags and things and took them up-stairs, and a little later Uncle Henson brought up on a silver tray one of those mint juleps, about which Father told Mr. Willie Prince, who made it, that the half could never be told, and at eight o'clock we had breakfast. Usually Father doesn't take anything at home but grape-fruit and coffee, but that morning, and every morning he was here, he ate waffles, and batter-bread, and beaten biscuits, and everything else Miss Susanna would urge him to try, and he said he couldn't understand how he could eat so much. I didn't tell him, but I think it was because of the juleps. They're the best things for poor appetites ever invented yet, Major Hairston says, and he ought to know, being over seventy and never having missed taking two a day since he could fix them for himself. After breakfast we talked for a while on the porch, and then I took Father out to show him the town.

I wouldn't have taken him out if the day had been hot, but it wasn't hot. It was one of those gorgeous days that sometimes come in summer after a thunder-storm and which have the feel and taste of early October; and being in the mountains it was cooler on that account, and I could see Father breathe deep, and the tiredness began to go away as we walked and talked. That is, I talked. He tried to at first, and then gave up. Everybody in town knew he was coming—I had told them—and they came down from their porches and shook hands with him, and said they were so glad to see him and they hoped he was going to stay some time, and that they would call as soon as he was rested, and a whole lot of other nice things, so that Father almost got flurried, he was so pleased and warmed up. At home he is always hurrying in the morning to get to the office, and at night hurrying to get away, and of course we don't have neighbors, and it was so queer to find everybody so friendly and interested that by the time we got back to Rose Hill he looked like another man.

CHAPTER X

I took him down Princess Street first, of course, and showed him the bank and post-office and moving-picture places, and the court-house and churches and stores, and specially the drug-store, which is a sort of standing-up club for the men; and I told him whose were the offices; and Whythe came out of his and spoke to him in a perfectly perfect way, and said he hoped he would be permitted to show him some of the things of interest in the neighborhood. And also he said if it was convenient to us he would call in a car (Whythe hasn't even a Ford, but he has a Twin-Six manner) in the morning and we would drive to Horseshoe Falls, and from there go on to Spruce Mountain, where something historic happened during the Revolution, I think; and only once when talking did he look right in my eyes. His sent a message, and my heart flopped around so it felt like a frog in a can of milk, and, I was so afraid Father would hear, I told Whythe we would go with pleasure and were much obliged, but we couldn't stop any longer, as there was a good deal to see before dinner. He shook hands twice with Father, who, when he was out of hearing, asked me how a young man could leave his business in the morning and go riding. I told him business could always be left in Twickenham Town, and he laughed and said he wished he lived in a town of that sort. I wish he did.

We stopped just a minute to speak to Mr. Bugg, who sells vegeta-bles and eggs and things, and whose wife has just had twins again, and this time has a milk-leg also, and Father shook hands with him and asked about the babies, I thinking just in time to tell him to do it, and then we had some soda-water at Mrs. Grump's. It is the most awful soda-water in the world, Mrs. Grump's is, but it is wet and cold, and you can sit down when drinking it, and while we sat she touched up the town and Father nearly fell out of his chair at the way she did it. If Mrs. Grump were for sale, I'd sell everything I own to get enough to buy her, for the way she can put into words what she thinks of human beings would make a graven image come to life. She never smiles herself.

After we got through with Princess Street we turned in by Colonel Rixby's and then went down by the Baconses' and into The Court, whose trees were planted by order of some lordly person, kin to the Aikens who have been sitting under the shade of their greatness ever since, and then we strolled by the Eppes house, for I wanted Father to see it. It is the stateliest old place in town and its garden of old-fashioned flowers makes one think the twentieth century is a mistake and ought never to have been, but ordinarily I pass it quickly, as I don't care for its owners. The house has perfect lines and the dearest little panes of glass in its deep, wide windows; and inside it has big fireplaces and beautifully carved woodwork and wonderful old furniture and fearful old portraits, and I certainly wanted Father to see everything in it, but I didn't expect him to do it, for the House of Eppes doesn't admire me any more than I admire it—and then the unexpected happened.

As we reached the gate we saw the whole bunch sitting in the wide, cool hall—Sister reading aloud, Sister Edwina making tatting, and Miss Lily Lou peeling a peach for Mother from a basket on the table beside her, and I was going to pass by and just bow to Mother as pleasantly and politely as I could (she was the only one who saw us), when to my surprise she got up and ordered me to stop by a wave of her hand. I stopped. She does not approve of me. She thinks it very indelicate in me to accept the attentions of one whose engagement had so recently been broken, and, while she will never recover from stupefaction that Elizabeth should disagree with her son, she attributed that action on Elizabeth's part to lack of sense and does not hesitate to say so, just as she has not hesitated to say things about me that were not as Christian as they might have been. She knew, however, what was expected of Twickenham Town and that personal feelings were to be paid no attention to where politeness was concerned, and with a sort of scepter movement she beckoned to me and commanded us to come in. We went.

It is a queer thing how nice disagreeable people can be when they want to, and that morning the entire Eppes family (even Sister Edwina, who's the limit) were so polite and pleasant that Father never would have imagined how cocky and sniffy they usually are. I behaved as well as they did, and when we came away I couldn't remember a thing I had said that I shouldn't. We didn't stay but half an hour. I wouldn't have held out a whole hour, and neither would they, and so, after we had seen all the beautiful old things downstairs and been introduced to all the painted ancestors, I got away quick, for Miss Anna was showing signs I didn't think were safe. They don't know that they worship idols of wood and glass and silver and china, and images in old gilt frames, but they do, and the steel trust hasn't money enough to buy them. It's a pity they won't sell a few and put the money in some new clothes, for those they wear are a sight to behold. As we were leaving, Mother Eppes invited us to take dinner with her on Sunday in a way that was more a command than an invitation and we accepted in a manner to match, though inside I was raging to think we'd have to go. And then I remembered it would be a regular thriller to be eating at the table with Whythe and his family and my family, and I hoped I'd remember to call him Mr. Eppes, as down here they do that up to the day of the marriage, the first name being thought too familiar until after the ceremony, and even then in public. Grace Marvin, who is engaged to Richard Clarke, calls him Dick, but that is because she isn't ancestral; just accepted, Mrs. Grump says, and she knows, being familiar with the history of everybody in town.

They were perfect days, the four Father spent in Twickenham Town, and he was made over when he went away. Every morning Mr. Willie Prince sent him up a mint julep that started the day so cheerfully he was happy through its every minute; and Major Roke, who makes the best ones in town, would come for him at twelve o'clock and take him to his house, and Mr. Letcher always managed to get hold of him about six in the afternoon, and at bedtime some one else would send one in. And poor Father, who never drinks anything at home, it not being good for him, was in an awful state of mind at first, and then he decided he would rather die than hurt the feelings of the senders and he'd take the chance on his health. He took.

I'm a fighting disbeliever in whisky, and if I had any say I'd say it couldn't be made except for sickness, but you couldn't get certain Twickenham-Towners to believe it is a dangerous thing, and to take a little something for the stomach's sake is a recommendation in the Bible they approve of and obey. It doesn't seem to kill people here or some would have been a long time dead, but there are one or two it is a pity it hasn't killed. It does much worse than kill; it ruins. I hope next time Father will say the doctor doesn't permit him to touch anything. I didn't tell him so, of course, and I am afraid he will manage not to see the doctor before he leaves; but, anyhow, the morning and night juleps can be thrown out of the window after a sip to get the smell on if he wants to throw. I wouldn't take a bet that he will want, but I'm hoping.

I didn't see much of Whythe while Father was here—that is, by himself. He was awfully nice to Father and he liked him very much (Father liked Whythe, I mean), but he couldn't understand why he didn't get more of a move on and make business for himself. I told him in Twickenham Town people waited for business to come to them, and everybody knew Whythe was a lawyer, and if they need-ed his services they would let him know, and if they didn't there was no use waiting around, which was why he was out of his office so much of the time. And then Father asked me when I had heard from Billy and when he was coming home; and, thankful to change the subject, I told him all I knew and got out the cards and showed them to him.

We had so many things to talk about—Mother and the girls and the home people and things, and the people he had met in Twick-enham Town—that he hadn't talked about Billy, and when I showed him the cards he said Billy must have mighty little to do but write them, as there were fifty-six and he hadn't been gone but five weeks. He seemed to think that right many, so I didn't say anything much about his letters, which are long and once a week, but told him Billy would sail on September 16th, and get back before I did—that is, if I stayed until the 27th. He said I could if I wanted to, and that he would come down for the last week and take me back with him, and I was so happy I swirled him around in my arms and danced a dance I made up as I went along, and both Billy and Whythe Eppes were out of his mind when he stopped for breath. And that night he went away. Also that night I almost cried my eyes out for sorrow at his going and for gladness that he was my Father. I wonder if all girls love their fathers as I love mine!

CHAPTER XI

Billy has been pretty good about writing. Much better than I have been. I told him I would tell him all about Twickenham and the people, and what they did and how they did, and I intended to do it, but that is my chief trouble. I'm a grand intender and a poor doer. Billy never promises and always does. He sends cards from every place, he goes to, and a good many from the same place so I can see what he is seeing, which I couldn't do if he wrote a book of descriptions. He doesn't tell much about the cities and towns, most of which I have been in myself and am glad he leaves out, but he writes awfully interesting things about the places he pokes into by himself and the people he meets, and I almost die laughing over his accounts of his sister and a beau his mother has caught for her. She is a dandy-looking girl, his sister is, and wears the smartest clothes I ever saw except Florine's, and if Patricia has really landed a duke or a count or a thing of that sort, his mother will have a wedding that will fit the fellow all right. He's apt to be landed.

I never have understood how Billy was born of his parents. He cares no more for flum-foolishness than I do, which is why we have so much fun over the efforts certain mothers we know make to help their daughters get married, and we've decided to be failures as social successes and enjoy ourselves. My mother isn't at all like his mother. She is a precious mother, mine is, and adores Father and her children, but she is in the parade and has to keep step, not having courage to get out, and she thinks she must give her daughters every opportunity, and for daughters in Mother's world opportunity means marriage. Until she gets us settled she won't feel as if her duty had been done. That's why she has gone with Florine and Jessica to the same place Florine went to last summer with the Logans. Florine has had a good many beaux, but none of them has been just what she had set her mind on, and last summer she met a man I believe she fell in love with. Anyhow, she has gone where it will be convenient for him to see her if he wants to, and he must want, as Mother says in every one of her letters that Mr. Jeffry has just come or just gone. He came to see Florine last winter, and a blind person could tell he was worth having. I hope they will take each other. Mother would be so pleased. Jessica and I are not apt to do much for ourselves in the marrying line, so it is left to Florine to make the catch.

She is very beautiful, Florine is. She knows it and she loves beautiful things and wouldn't think of marrying any one who could not give them to her. She wouldn't marry a man who isn't decent and straight and all that, not being that kind, but neither is she romantic, and nothing on earth could make her lose her head. She is cool and deliberate and far-seeing, and not apt to ask herself too many questions about love alone when thinking about marriage. She is a dream to look at, which Jessica isn't, but I love Jessica best.

Last night in bed I got to thinking about old Jess, and wondering how she was making out with that bunch up there, and I almost rolled out at the way her nose must be turning up inside of her at some of the things she was seeing and hearing and had to take part in; and I laughed so loud that Miss Susanna came in my room to see if anything were the matter. I told her no, and that I was just thinking of something, so she pattered back, and I put my face in the pillow to keep her from hearing me again. But it was hard not to let it come out. Mother's daughters are a mixture all right, and no more alike than if they weren't related to one another. Being a parent must be an anxious job. I hope I will have a dozen children, but they'll probably be right much to manage. If I turn out to be a childless old maid, I'll adopt a boy and girl, anyhow. I can do that if I can't do anything else.

Jessica is the clever one of our family. Florine has the beauty and Jessica the brains, and so far nothing has shown signs in me, but something may turn up yet. Jessica is an A.M., and she has Ideas and Views and Opinions which she isn't stingy with and lets anybody have who is within hearing, and she wanted to be something, have a Career and get an Identity, which she says a woman has no chance of doing as long as she sinks herself in marriage; but Father said she couldn't go to any more colleges until she had had a fling at fun, for it wasn't fair to Mother. She came out last winter and had a fearful rush because she was so different from the other girls.

I don't believe Jessica would ever have wasted a winter doing the things she did last year if she hadn't wanted to see for herself what was in it, anyhow, in society I mean, so she took a header and plunged all right. She says she has a scientific and analytical mind and she worked it all out—the number of hours and days and weeks and months she had spent flopping around from one party to another, and doing the things she was supposed to do, and saying the things she wasn't supposed to say, and then she estimated the cost in time and strength and money and wear and tear on her character, and announced that it wasn't a paying business, and at the end of the year she was going to get out. The year won't be up until October and that is why she is with Mother and Florine this summer.

What she is going in for when it is up I don't believe she knows herself, yet. She says woman to-day is in the most unsettled and uncertain state that any animal has ever been in since the first one, a mollusk, or something without a backbone started to get one. And that it will take time for woman to evolute into being the best kind of a human being she is capable of becoming, and that the next step in the evoluting is to get out of her head some of the foolishness put in it by men people who didn't know what they were talking about. Mother thinks it fearful in her to talk as she does, and can't understand how she can be so daring and so indelicate as to speak about coming from mollusks and things which don't have spinal columns and nervous systems, but Jessica says that is because Mother belongs to a day that didn't know about such things, and that the modern woman is shedding the shucks which have kept her a caterpillar much longer than was necessary. A good many old ideas she thinks are shucks—that is, she pretends to; but she is an old dear just the same, if she does say things about people which it isn't polite to say.

I love old Jess. She isn't but twenty-two, and she will be less sniffy some of these days and not so scornful and impatient with repeaters and parasiters and people like that, but just now she says they aren't worth wasting time on. She can talk you right into seeing her way, and the first thing you know you are agreeing with her, and she has landed you before you realized the net was out. Landed outsiders, I mean. She will never land Mother and Florine. I love to hear her talk, though I don't think I am going to be a Careering person. I'd like to be one, but with a dozen children I am afraid there won't be time. I wouldn't tell old Jess, but I don't think she is going to Career very long, either. I believe she is in love with the man who taught her some of the ologies she is so interested in. He is awfully nice, but not very practical. He is a psychological sociologist or a sociological psychologist, I don't know which, but it doesn't matter. If Jess marries him she will run him and the house.

CHAPTER XII

I wonder what made me get on the subject of my sisters when I began with Billy and the reason I had not written him as often as he has written me, but that is the way I do everything in life. If I were a preacher I wouldn't hold my job long, for the thing I started on would have about as much connection with the thing I ended with as the moon with milk. Not that that would be unusual, for a good many ministers have the same failing and skip about just as I do, but my trouble would be in hopping from one subject to another so fast that the congregation would be in Jericho one minute and in Jerusalem the next and never know how it made the jump. As I am never going to be a preacher, I am not worrying about my unfitness to be one, but what does worry me sometimes is that my hopping habit will be my ruination when I begin to write a book. My characters will never keep together, or do the proper things or say suitable ones. They will probably get so jumbled up no one will be able to tell which is the chief hero or heroine, and there will be no logical development at all, which my English teacher insists is an elemental requirement of fiction if it isn't of life. I thought this summer I was going to begin some sort of book just for practice, but by the time I get through putting down the things I scribble about the day's doings, and write to Father and send my weekly letter to Mother and the girls, and run off something every now and then to Billy, and answer the notes I get from Whythe and some of the kiddies around here who think they're grown, I don't feel like writing on a book, which is why I haven't begun one yet. I will never be able to write one that tells of dark deeds and treacherous doings and love-sick lovers, or one which has suspended interest or rapid action and narrow escapes, for I know very little of such things, and I will never do much with plots. The people I know do not have very exciting lives and here in Twickenham they trot along and do the same thing over and over, and one day is very much like the other, so there isn't much inspiration for a thriller, and thrillers are the style in books to-day. That is one reason I thought I had better wait until the style changes and while waiting enjoy myself with the people here who know how to do that better than any people on earth. I'm enjoying myself all right.

Of course, now that I am in love, I could write volumes on how scrumptious it is and how floppy I feel whenever I see Whythe, especially when he keeps his deep, dark eyes on me as if he were trying to read my soul when we happen to meet at the foot of the hill and sit on the worm fence for a while. I don't think he is trying to really read my soul, for he isn't much on reading anything, but he certainly can say beautiful things. They aren't so, but they sound well, and I must admit I enjoy hearing them. They make me feel so grown-upy, and then, too, it will be a great help when I begin my book to remember what a man says on certain occasions and how he says it. They are natural couriers, the men in this town are, but they don't always mean to be taken in earnest, and Mr. James Burke came near getting in an awful mess by paying a girl a lot of compliments he oughtn't to have paid, he being a married man and she not knowing it. She was a very serious person and believed all that was told her and came near breaking her engagement with another man on account of the pretty speeches Mr. Burke made to her. She was from Rhode Island and visiting May Strudwick, who told her for mercy's sake not to pay any attention to speeches of that sort and to hold on to the Rhode-Islander, for Mr. Burke said the same fluff to all the girls who came to Twickenham, and as long as it was just eyebrows and things of that kind no harm was done. But she couldn't understand and went home sooner than she expected. I understand. It's lots of fun—the different ways of saying the same thing—and all enlightenment is advantageous.

A few nights ago Whythe got fearfully sentimental and said all sorts of thrilly, foolish nonsense, and the way he said it certainly added to its enjoyment. He's a corking courter, and if he could teach the way he does it he would have crowded classes all right. We were at Bessie Debree's party, and just before supper we went out on the side porch, which has bushels of roses on it and no lights, and sat down on a rustic bench in the corner where we could hear the music and see the moon and not be seen, and the minute we sat I knew what was coming.

Whythe put his elbow on the back of the seat and, chin in the palm of his hand, looked at me as if we were on a desert island and there was no one else in all the world but me, and he would ask for no one else if I alone was there; and then with his other hand he tried to take out of my fingers a rose he had just pulled and given me. I remembered in time that Jess had told me to keep my hands to myself if anybody seemed interested in them, so I put the rose on the bench and sat on my hands and asked him if he did not think Marjorie Graham a perfectly beautiful person; and he said he hadn't noticed her sufficiently to know what she looked like, as he never saw but one face now. And then he leaned a little closer and asked me if I knew how wonderful I was and what my eyes could do to a man's heart if I would only let come in them what could come, and which he hoped would some day come only for him; and I asked him what it was, not knowing, as it had never been mentioned before, and he said it was a thing a man would die for. And then he took the rose up and put it to his lips and asked me if I would marry him; asked me if I could never care for him as he cared for me, for he knew now that he had never really loved before, and if I would promise to marry him he would be in heaven, his happiness would be so great.

It was perfectly thrilling, much better than anything I have ever seen on the stage. He tried to get one of the hands I was still sitting on, but I thought I had better not let him have it, as we were not engaged, and Jess had said no affectionaries until you are engaged. And then, too, I remembered he had probably said the same things several times before, he seemed so familiar with them, and I had a feeling that Billy was standing by, perfectly disgusted, but ready to fish me out if I fell in. I came pretty near falling, and then I told Whythe I wouldn't be through college until I was twenty and I didn't believe in waiting for anything on earth for four years, and though it was awfully nice in him to ask me to marry him, my father would have fits if he thought I was listening to him do it, and that we had better go in.

I wish I had had a kodak and could have snapped the look that came over his face when I suggested going in. He was perfectly astonished. Also he was indignant and grieved and the look he bent upon me was truly burning. As for his voice—Sothern couldn't have surpassed it. After a while he said he thought I had more sympathy, more understanding of a love such as his, and if I realized its depth I would not keep him waiting four years, as four years at college was all nonsense for a woman; and then he got my hand, anyhow, and I jumped up, for somebody was coming, and, besides, if we hadn't gone in we'd have been in an argument right off, with love left out, on the subject of education and women. I did not want him to think I was not appreciative, however, and though I went in with Mr. Keane, who had come for his dance, I gave Whythe a little look that was not unfriendly as I left him. I am afraid it was not even discouraging, but he seemed so mysterious and tragic and amazed that I should leave him at such a critical time that I thought a little look wouldn't hurt. I noticed, as we reached the door, that he was lighting a cigarette, and I knew his feelings would soon be soothed. Man has no sorrow that smoking may not cure.

When we went home that night other people were in the automobile (I always see that that happens, knowing how Mother would feel about it) and Whythe, of course, had no chance to continue a former conversation, but his silence said a lot, and when he helped me out of the car he helped much more than was necessary and held my hands so tight he nearly broke my little finger; and the look he gave me was a thriller all right. Every time I've thought of it since my heart has thumped so I know I must be in love, for all books say that is a reliable symptom. Being proposed to is awfully interesting, and the reason I like it so much is that I am not apt to have many proposals of Whythe's sort, as that kind has gone out of fashion, owing to golf and tennis and country clubs and so much association. Plain statement is about all a girl gets nowadays, I am told. Jacqueline Smith told Florine Mr. Smith had wired her he had to go to South America and asked her if she would marry him and go with him, and she wired back she would, and that was all the courting they had, though they seem very happy. And a girl Jess knows said the man she married had asked her how he stood with her, that she stood all right with him, and that was the way they knew they cared for each other. But I'm not that sort. I am very romantic and I like a lot of words, which is why I am just crazy about Whythe's letters.

If Whythe doesn't make a success of law or politics he could certainly make a living writing letters of a certain sort. He's an expert at them and greatly gifted, and though I don't say much in mine, thinking it safer to telephone than write, I do tell him that his are perfectly lovely, at which he doesn't seem displeased. He still begs me to marry him, and is so fearfully polite about it that I don't like to ask him what he has to marry on, and so far as I know he has only nerve and his mother's home. I would not like to spend eternity as a maiden lady, but I'd much rather so spend it than dwell under the vine and fig-tree of the person who would be a mother-in-law to Whythe's wife. My heart goes out to Elizabeth every time I think of the fate that will eventually be hers. Also it goes out to the House of Eppes. When opposing elements meet something usually happens. I'm betting on Elizabeth, but I may be wrong.

CHAPTER XIII

Jehoshaphat the Golden! For two days Twickenham Town has been standing on its head and wriggling its heels in the air, and nothing has been talked about since it appeared except its appearance. Every tongue in town has had its say, and everybody in town has been on somebody else's porch and talked it over; and as for Miss Susanna, I believe she cried the whole night through, last night. The first night she was too dazed to take it in. The Twickenham Town *Sentinel* had it on its front page in the middle column in letters indecently large, Miss Bettie Simcoe says, and it certainly did make a sensation: "Mrs. Roger S. Payne announces the engagement of her niece Elizabeth Hamilton Carter to Mr. Algernon Grice Baker, of Perryville, Wisconsin," was what the Twickenham-Towners waked up and read on Wednesday the 1st of August, and if the dynamite-plant which has made business so good for Buzzard

Brothers, the undertakers, had exploded, it couldn't have caused more of a stir. Twickenham wasn't only amazed; it was indignant, and it couldn't believe it was true. But it was true, for the next day Miss Susanna got a letter from Elizabeth, telling her all about her engagement and that she would be home very soon and bring him with her, and it was the night of the day the letter was received that Miss Susanna went early to her room and locked her door for a while (that is, my door, for she is sleeping in my room during the August rush) and cried all night long. I had to pretend I didn't know, for she didn't want me to know how hurt and distressed she was that Elizabeth should have so treated her, and as I didn't sleep any more than she did, though, owing to very different feelings about Elizabeth, I made up my mind as to some things I would say to her when she got back. And if she has never read "King Lear" I will see that she hears it read before very long with a glossary, and comments of my own on ingratitude and things of that sort. Also she may hear some other things.

I have been perfectly furious with Elizabeth for the way she has treated the aunt who has been mother and father and all things else to her, but I can't help laughing at the way Twickenham Town has taken the engagement.

As for Whythe—I have wished for Billy a dozen times of late, for only Billy could see what a scream it is, the shock to Whythe's vanity that Elizabeth's beau is proving. I can't speak of it to any one else, and keeping it to myself is a great strain. At first he seemed dazed with unbelief, and then he became scorny and sniffy and shruggy and smiley, and though he says little about his successor, whom he hasn't seen yet, his manner indicates that as a substitute for himself he considers him an insult.

Last night at the gate he talked to me about it for a while, and then he asked me when I was going to tell him I would marry him, and why was it I would not engage myself to him and take him out of his miserable state of uncertainty and make him the happiest man in the world, and why— Oh, my granny! he spieled it off so beautifully and his eyes helped so wonderfully, also the moon, which was half out and half in, that I stayed a little longer at the gate than I should, perhaps, and let him say things he shouldn't, but his fluency was so enjoyable I couldn't get away. After a while, however, when he had run down a little, I told him I didn't think it would be respectful to what might have been if I engaged myself to him, and that sixteen was too young to be engaged, and then, too, it wasn't positively certain that a certain young person was going to marry another young person just because she was at present engaged to him. At which he got perfectly furious and said he would not marry that certain person if she was the only woman left on earth; that she had treated him as no lady should treat a gentleman, and that she was vain and mercenary and ambitious, and he was mortified to think he had ever imagined he had loved so shallow and weak and changeable a girl, and—

"But you did love her, didn't you?" I got up on the gate-post, swung my feet down, and put my hands in my lap and out of reach, the post not being big enough for two. "Everybody says you were frightfully in love with her and you didn't think she was shallow and weak and mercenary until you had the break, and maybe you may change your mind back again about her some day, and then where would I be?" I put my chin in my hands and my elbows in my lap and looked down at him, and he looked so hurt and surprised that I saw he had not thought of his own real gift for changing, and I realized that his attention ought to be drawn to some things he was apt to forget. Quick as a flash, though, he said I had opened new worlds to him; that I stimulated and inspired him as no one had ever done, and that he would never love any one as he loved me, and that he would wait forever if necessary for me. Also he said he would never change back again to a certain person, as she had killed his love, and would I not promise to be just his? And I had to sit tight on my hands, his manner was so very imploring; and then, before I could say anything, I heard Mr. Willie Prince, who was sitting on the front porch, fanning, cough rather loud and come down the steps and call Ben, who was barking, and I knew Mr. Willie was doing what he thought was his duty, and I got down from the post and told Whythe good night. He went away like the young man in the Bible, very sorrowful, and I went in.

It wasn't late, but everybody had gone in except Miss Susanna and Mr. Willie, and when I sat down in a rocking-chair Miss Susanna looked at me as if she didn't know whether to say anything or not, and I saw she was worried. But before I could ask what was the matter she got up and kissed me good night and went in, so I asked Mr. Willie.

He wouldn't tell me at first, though I could see he was dying to do it, but after a while he said Miss Susanna was the sort that found life of the present day a hard thing to accept, and, fanning himself with his palm leaf, he looked at me as if I were one of the reasons she found life hard. "Miss Susanna," he said, "is a lady of the old school where love and honor were placed above riches and mere material things, and it was a blow to her to find how readily young people could change their affections and break their plighted vows and be blind to their best interests, which was to keep along the same path and not be tempted out of it by passing people and worldly ambitions." And as he talked in his fine little cambric-needle voice that sounded as if it came out of a squeaky cabinet, I knew he was meaning more than he was saying, and I sat up and listened until he stopped for breath.

"Is that all?" I asked, and got up to go in, "for if it is I don't think Miss Susanna need worry herself. People in one generation aren't very different from people in another where self-interest is concerned. Everybody knows Mrs. Loraine married her husband for his money, though loving Mr. Spence, and Miss Susanna was one of her bridesmaids; and if Elizabeth prefers to marry a rich man to a poor one, I don't see anything new about that." And also I said it wasn't likely that love and honor were ever going to die out, and a few other things would live a long time yet, and he need not bother any more than Miss Susanna concerning present-day young people; and then to my surprise he asked me to sit down and told me what he enjoyed telling very much.

CHAPTER XIV

"Everybody has been talking about the way Whythe Eppes has been rushing you," he began, fanning as hard as he could fan, "and several people have been to see Miss Susanna and told her they thought your parents ought to know —"

He didn't get any further. I stopped him. It was silly in me to get hot, but I got hot all right, and in all my life I never wanted anybody as I wanted Billy right then at my side. He doesn't get mad the way I do. He would see that talk he did not like was stopped in two minutes, but I was too fighting angry to stop my own tongue, and I said things to fat Miss Nancy Willie Prince I oughtn't to have said. Among them that my parents would not have permitted me to come to this town or any other if not perfectly certain I knew how to behave myself wherever I went, and that whatever was advisable for them to know concerning me they would know without the assistance of Miss Bettie Simcoe or Mrs. Caperton (she is a frisky little widow who has no use for young girls) or any other Twicken-ham-Towner. And then, perhaps because he was so flustered he didn't know what he was saying, he told me riches were a great temptation to any young man, and everybody, of course, knew my father was wealthy, though he must say it had not been learned from the family. And that Whythe, being poor from a money stand-point, had naturally been tempted, especially as his engagement had been so recently broken with a girl he had been in love with since childhood, and I, being young, didn't understand and was under the impression that young men meant all they said, and—

He would be talking now if I had not stamped my foot and stopped his rambling. His insinuations sounded as if I were a fee-ble-minded creature and couldn't tell truth from untruth, or know when a man meant or didn't mean what he said, and had never heard things of the same sort before. I've heard them before, and in several different places. I am a good many things I ought not to be, but I am not feeble-minded. I told him— It does not matter what I told him, but I made him understand I could take care of myself without the help of the town, and, while I appreciated his effort to keep me from thinking the men in Twickenham did not mean what they said, and were not to be relied on, and not to be trusted, and that honor was not held very high by them where young girls were concerned, it was difficult to believe it, for I had been made to un-derstand by others that certain old-fashioned things were still held sacred there, and the dangers and temptations of the city were ab-sent. When I saw how red his fat, round face got and how squirmy his legs and how hard he fanned I knew I had better go in. I went, but I didn't say good night.

Mad! Was I mad? I was. For a long time I sat by the window and talked to Billy in my mind and told him what I thought of men old-maids and prissy places and gossipy spinsters and flirtatious widows, and of people who didn't have anything to talk of but one another; and then, as the moon came out clearer, I seemed to see myself clearer also, and after a while it came over me that maybe I had been a little nicer to Whythe than was necessary just to see if a man couldn't get comforted sooner than he thought. I had been doing a little scientific experimenting along a different way from Jess's way; and then my eyes got open wide and I saw what Mr. Willie had been trying to tell me, which was that Whythe was probably taking practical consolation and was not ignorant of the fact that my Father was not a poor man.

At the thought something got into my backbone and I sat up. I had been fooling myself and didn't know it. I don't mean I had believed all the thrilly love things Whythe had been saying. They came natural to him and he might have said them to some other girl if not to me, but I had not dreamed he had any thought of an advantageous alliance, as Billy calls the thing his mother is hoping his sister will make, or that any one could associate such a thought with me. It didn't seem possible, and I don't believe Whythe is that sort. Still, men are queer ducks, Jess says, and one never can tell what is in the back of their brain from the words of their mouth, and if Whythe was imagining I had any value outside of my own self I would like to find it out. How I was going to find out I did not know, and when I said my prayers I started to pray that a rattling good way would turn up, but I remembered it wasn't exactly a thing to pray about and that watching might be better.

I had had a grand time being in love. Every day there was some new evidence of how nice a beau is, and though the other boys didn't let Whythe have it all his own way, as they called it, and we had a jolly time together and I danced and rode and picnicked and pleasured with all of them, still, it was understood that Whythe was my steady and they gave him right much chance. It had been loads of fun having a steady, and I knew now how excited Mazie, one of our maids at home, must have felt the day she became engaged to hers, who was the milkman. But I had somehow thought that nobody but girls of Mazie's sort had steadies, and I had wished I could be a maid for a few weeks just to find out how it would feel to possess some one and be possessed by him. I guess it amounts to about the same thing, though, love does, no matter in what way it comes to one or by what name we call it, if it is the genuine thing. I have certainly never felt about Whythe in the way Mazie must have felt about her milkman, judging by her face, but I had been enjoying myself and I didn't intend to stop with too much suddenness. Mr. Willie had warned me and I would remember, but it is against the law to condemn a man unheard. The Bible says so. I would go slowly for once in my life and give Whythe a chance to conduct his own defense. It wouldn't be necessary to mention that a case was being tried or that I would be both judge and jury. There are times in life when it is well to keep some things to oneself.

CHAPTER XV

Yesterday it poured in torrents all day. None of us could get out of the house, so while Miss Araminta darned my stockings, which hadn't been touched since I came to Twickenham Town, I read aloud to the whole bunch in the library and we had a very nice time. Miss Araminta has tried to teach me to darn since I have been here, but she has not succeeded in doing it! I will never be a darner. I have asked Mother not to get me all-over silk stockings, as the Lisle-thread feet last much longer, but she doesn't seem to remember, and one of my charities is giving my nice stockings away when they can no longer be worn with self-respect. Clarissa, Mother's maid, is supposed to keep them in order, but she doesn't do it, and she has headaches so often I don't like to say anything to her, with the result that Mother thinks I wear out an awful lot, and yet I know she wouldn't want me to wear stockings with holes in them. I found out early in life that it is foolish to try to do things you are not by nature fitted to do, and I am not fitted by nature to sit still for hours and fill up a little hole in a stocking to save a few cents or a dollar or so. I don't do it. I would rather save in some other way.

Miss Araminta loves to darn. Also she loves pretty clothes in a way that is truly pitiful, not having the means to get them, and she has about as much idea how to have her few things made as a Comanche Indian has of *vers-libre*. If she would wear those that suited her style she would look dear, but she wears clothes of many colors made, as she thinks, in the prevailing fashion, and of course she is a sight for all beholders. While I was reading *Pendennis* out loud I was wondering at the same time what Miss Araminta was going to wear to the reception Judge and Mrs. Maclean are going to give to their two married daughters and their husbands on the 17th of August, which is the big thing of the year for Twickenham Town; but of course I couldn't ask her. I knew she had nothing suitable or that had not been the subject of nudges and remarks under the breath, and smiles that could be heard. And I also knew nothing could keep her away, for she dearly loves to go to parties and is not often invited, being of an inconvenient age for entertainments, and I wished something could come to pass that would be to her interest.

As I read I poked around in my mind trying to think what might be done, and suddenly something came to me, and after a while I put the book down and began to talk of the different things that were going on in town and the many visitors who were already there, and then I asked Miss Araminta if she didn't think lavender was a lovely color. She said it was the one she loved best and all her life she had longed for a lavender satin with everything to match, but she knew now she would never have it and she rarely let herself wish for things any more. And she sighed the softest little sigh, like a mother whose baby had died a long time ago, but who always kept it in her heart, and I said to myself, "Go up-stairs, Kitty Canary, and think out a way," and up-stairs I went.

August is The Season in Twickenham Town, and there is hardly a family in it that doesn't have company or boarders, or whose sons and daughters don't come home for their holiday, and Miss Bettie Simcoe says it's perfectly scandalous, the flirting that goes on. Miss Bettie thinks anything matrimonial is close to scandalous, and she is continually raising her eyebrows and making a half moon of her mouth at what she says is the forwardness and freeness of present-day young people. Miss Susanna always has a crowded house in August. A Doctor Macafee and his wife and two daughters are here from Florida, and a Miss LeRoy from New Hampshire, and Judge Lampton and his wife from Alabama, and how she manages to put them away is known only to herself.

When I heard she was going to give up her room and take a tiny one in the garret I made up my mind I would have an awful dream that night, a regular nightmare, that would scare her to death and make her come in my room to see what was the matter. I had it and she came, and I told her I was subject to nightmares and ought not to sleep in a room by myself, though I hadn't mentioned it before, and I wished she would please sleep in mine with me and take the four-poster, which I thought gave me bad dreams, as I wasn't accustomed to such high beds. And if she would I would take the cot, as I liked cots much better. I am subject to nightmares, or anything else that is advisable to have at the proper time, and if I had known how many people were coming and that Miss Susanna was going to give up her room, I would have had one before, so she wouldn't think they had come on pretty sudden. But she is not apt to think. She is a darling little old lady, not brought up to think, and now too busy to do it, and she just works herself to death with her head up and a smile on her face, and doesn't realize she is spending all she makes in good things for the people who come here and nearly kill themselves eating. She never buys herself any clothes—that is, until Elizabeth has all she needs—and when I went up to my room yesterday to think out a way of getting that lavender satin for Miss Araminta, another thought came into my head, which was a black satin for Miss Susanna.

Feelings are things one has to be awfully careful about in Twickenham Town, and not for a billion dollars put in my pocket would I hurt anybody's here, and I couldn't let Miss Araminta or Miss Susanna think for a moment that their dresses were not all right, and how to get them new ones I couldn't imagine. I started to pray about it, and then I remembered I was in an awful hurry and it would be better to get to work, and, going over to the bureau, I opened its top drawer, and there looking up at me was my bank-book lying on a pile of handkerchiefs. Father had put a very respectable sum of money in the Twickenham bank for me and told me to use it whenever I could do it in the right way, and he would trust me to find the right way; but though I had tried to get rid of some of it, there were few opportunities (so it wouldn't be manifest, I mean), and now one popped right up in my face.

For fear it might pop out again I ran downstairs as quick as I could, and, seeing Miss Susanna and Miss Araminta were by themselves, I began to talk about the Pettigrew children and what they had told me they wanted Santa Claus to bring them Christmas. And that reminded me suddenly that Christmas would soon be here, and I told them that in August I always began to think about what to get Mother and Aunt Celeste, who were my chief Christmas worries, and I wondered if they thought I could get something in Twickenham that I could take back with me. I felt, as I talked, that I was on a tight rope forty feet in the air and mighty little to balance myself with, but I managed to put in words what I wanted to say, and like little angels they fell in and never dreamed I had thought the thing out before I spoke.

I told them that Mother and Aunt Celeste had much more than they needed in life, and it was hard to get anything new and different for them, as there were so many to give them presents, and that I liked to get something odd if I could. The things they were crazy about were old silver and old jewelry, especially old settings, and it was hard to find them in our town, and I wondered if they could help me get a piece of silver like one of Miss Susanna's pitchers for Mother, and a set of sapphires like Miss Araminta's for Aunt Celeste. Also I said I didn't want to trouble them and I hoped they wouldn't mind my asking them.

Miss Araminta said no indeed, she didn't mind, and that she had got into the state of mind Miss Virginia Hill was in, and she wasn't going to keep on keeping a lot of things that were no use just because they had belonged to long-dead grandmothers. And while she wouldn't go as far as Miss Virginia, who would sell every ancestor she had for a million dollars, she would part with some other things for much less, and if I wanted to buy the sapphire set (pin and ear-rings) she would be glad to sell them. She would have to tell me, though, they had been her great-grandmother's, and not her great-great's, as the pearls were, and that she would take forty-five dollars for them, and if that was too much she would take forty.

I almost lost my breath at her good sense, not expecting it, but I told her it would be cheating if I paid less than seventy-five for them (I had calculated that it would take about that to get the lavender satin with things to match), and if she would get them for me I would take them right away, and I was awfully obliged to her, as it would be such a relief to get Aunt Celeste off my mind. I admitted I didn't always pay as much as seventy-five for her present (I usually give her a five-dollar one which Mother pays for), but Father wanted me to bring her something quaint from Twickenham if I could find it, and he would be delighted to know of the sapphires.

I fiddled along about other things for a moment or two and then I asked Miss Susanna if she would think me a very piggy person to want to buy one of those precious old silver pitchers of hers, as Mother would love so to have one of that pattern (Mother had never mentioned it, but I knew she would long for one of that pattern if she could see it), and I waited with terrible anxiousness in my heart and a hot face for her answer. Miss Susanna's got a lovely pinky color, and for a moment she didn't say anything, and then Miss Araminta spoke for her and showed more sensibleness than I thought was in her.

"Why don't you, Susanna?" she said, and nodded at her. They are first cousins and very good friends. "Why don't you let the child have one of those old pitchers? You have too much silver, anyhow, and with servants of the present day any sort of silver is too great a burden to be borne, much less ancestral sort. Young people want to buy their own things, and reverence for the past is a thing of the past; and besides, you have no one to leave yours to except some one who won't appreciate it. Why don't you let her have it?"

"I would be glad for her to have it. Glad to help her out with her Christmas difficulties, but"—Miss Susanna bit her lip and the pink in her face became rose—"I have never done anything of this sort, and it does not seem just right. I would be pleased for her mother to have one of the pitchers. In a sense they are connected with her family as our great-great-great-grandmothers were the same, and—"

"Oh, you precious person!" I jumped up and took Miss Susanna in my arms and whirled around the room with her. I was afraid she would get on the grandparent subject, and I didn't want to hear it. To head her off I gave her a squeeze and a skip or two and then I sat her down and kissed her, and asked her if she thought seventy-five dollars was enough for the pitcher, and if so I would get the checks while Miss Araminta got the sapphires. And before they had time to change their minds their things were mine and my money (Father's) was theirs, and we were all a little more excited than we were willing to admit.

CHAPTER XVI

They are in my trunk, the two Christmas presents, and we have had a grand time, Miss Araminta and Miss Susanna and I, buying their party dresses and things, and it is as true as Scripture that at times there is nothing better for the soul than pretty clothes for the body. And nothing so chirps up a woman as to have on becoming ones that fit and are fresh and make her feel she can walk across the floor without wishing she had a shawl on. The way Miss Araminta has bloomed out is as amazing as a moon-plant. And Miss Susanna has such a pleased smile on her boarder-tired face that I have been up in the air just from looking at her, and the best time I've ever had in my life has been in taking charge of their money and spending it for them. The way they agreed to get the dresses was this:

I told them it would be awfully exciting to have a secret and spring a surprise on Mrs. General Gaines and Miss Bettie Simcoe and a few others in town, and if they were willing I would design a dress for each of them and Miss Fannie Cross would make the dresses, which would be of a kind to suit their particular styles, and they could have them for the party on the 17th. And if they didn't get them at once something would happen to make them spend the money and it would be gone and they no better off than before. And I mentioned that there was the loveliest piece of black charmeuse at Mr. Peter Smith's, and that he was expecting a piece of lavender satin on Thursday. I had been to see Mr. Peter and the lavender was ordered before I told them it was coming. Also a few other things had been ordered by wire, I going with him to the telegraph-office to see him do it, being afraid to trust his memory, which, like his methods, is right put-offy. Also I told them there would be no time to hesitate. They got so flustrated at being managed and so dazed by the pictures I showed them of the dresses I had drawn that they were lambs, perfect lambs. They let me do everything I told them ought to be done.

It was a real relief to them to have some one go ahead and decide things and not give them time to think whether they should do this or do that, or whether they had not better spend the money some other way. Miss Susanna said, feebly, something about the roof needing to be fixed, and that the cellar ought to have a new floor, but I told her it would be sacrilegious to put a great-grandmother's silver pitcher on the roof or in the cellar, and that it would mortify her heavenly ancestors to know such a thing was being done, and I was surprised at her mentioning it. The only suitable way in which it would be proper to use the pitcher was in something personal, and as I was afraid Mr. Peter Smith would sell the satin, it was so lovely and only a little more than enough for a dress, I had told him to put it aside and I had to let him know that afternoon if it was wanted. And another thing I told her was that all her life other people had been getting her share of nice things, and practicalities had eaten up everything pretty she had wanted for years, and there was an end to making over, and that she owed it to memories of the past to have a new dress for herself and not let all the newness always appear on a certain person's back just because that certain person happened to be young. Uncle Henson would be at the door with the carriage at four o'clock, I told her, to take us down-town, and she must be ready in time, as there was a good deal to do. I wouldn't take a mint of money for the look that came in her face as I talked. I have put it away for low-down days.

As for Miss Araminta—I wish I could write a book and put Miss Araminta Armstrong in it. If the lady who wrote *Cranford* had known her she would have put her in, and it is a loss to literature that no one can do again for little places and the Miss Aramintas of life what the *Cranford* writer did. She has told me right much about herself, and I don't smile any more, even to myself, as I couldn't help doing at first in the dark when I was so afraid I would roll on the floor and whoop that I had to hold on to my chair with both hands. It is still funny to hear her tell of her beaux who never quite came to the point, and who were always snatched away at the critical moment by a jealous-minded person who was close kin but whose name she never mentions. But it isn't as funny as it used to be. It's queer how much tragedy there is in the comic things of life. Ever since she was born Miss Araminta has been a pieced-and-patched-up person, and never once has she had everything new and to match at the same time. When I told her about some of the things that must go with the lavender satin she began to cry a little and said she oughtn't to let herself think about indulgences of that sort, as her poor brother was not in business at present and needed—

"Now look here, Miss Araminta," I said. "The first preparation you have got to make for the party is to forget you have a brother and remember your own body, which needs attention. It has come down from a long line of people who took very good care to put expensive things on theirs. And another thing you ought to remember is that if your brother didn't know he could call on you every time he lost his job—"

"My brother has never had a job." Miss Araminta sat up at once and wiped her eyes and left, unknowing, a streak of white down a pink cheek that turned purple at the word "job." "He has been unfortunate in not being able to retain certain positions he has once held, but his health—"

"Rats!" It came out without thinking, but when a man has a worn-out wife and seven children and won't do this and won't do that because it is beneath his lordly ideas of what a well-born person should do, it is better for me not to speak of him out loud. I told Miss Araminta she must excuse me, but there were some sorts of men I couldn't mention with safety and I thought "job" was a very good word, and I would rather have one that paid a dollar a day than borrow money to pay my bills, and that I'd sweep the streets before I would sit down and do nothing if I had a wife and seven children. The look on her face I tucked away, too, to take out on days when there isn't a thing in sight to laugh at. She can't help it, Miss Araminta can't. She was born that way and, not being an evoluting kind, words are wasted when it comes to trying to make her see what she doesn't want to see. There is a lot of bummy rot in this world which has nothing to do with the proper kind of pride, and it's my belief we are mighty apt to fill the place in life we are fitted to fill. If a dollar a day is all I am worth it is all I ought to get until I make myself worth more. Of course if people are feeble-minded that's a different thing. When they are, the State ought to step in and take charge of them in order to protect itself, Jess says, and also she says feeble-mindeders always have the largest families, and even a feeble-minded person knows that is not right.

I didn't mean to hurt Miss Araminta's feelings, but that brother of hers is a snuff-the-moon old snob, and I was determined he shouldn't get a penny of that sapphire money if I could help it, and I told Miss Araminta a few firm facts. After a while she blew her nose and wiped her eyes and I had no further trouble. But I was afraid to trust either her or Miss Susanna with their money, so I took the checks back and told them it was better for me to keep them, as money had such a queer way of disappearing. Any that was handy was used when needed, and when the time came to get the things the money was for there might not be any to get. They handed it back as meek as little lambs.

CHAPTER XVII

Miss Susanna and Miss Araminta are crazy about the designs I have sketched for their dresses, and so is Miss Fannie Cross. It is the only talent I have, designing clothes is, and if I ever have to earn my living I am going to be "Katrine" and have a shop on a fine street and charge like old glory for my things. That will make them wanted, and those who think a gown is desirable according to its price can pay enough to make up for those who can't pay much, and I'll have a great time charging the payers. I am going to get ready to earn a living, anyhow, because every girl ought to, Fathers or Billys notwithstanding. Life is a very up-and-downy thing, and it is good to know, should it get down, that you can give it a lift up yourself and not have to wait for a shover.

It was a private matinée, watching Miss Susanna and Miss Araminta buy the things that Mr. Peter Smith had ordered and which they couldn't understand his having in stock. The trimmings and linings and gloves and stockings were exactly what was needed and they couldn't get over how fortunate it was. They paid for them themselves, as I had handed their money to them when we started out, holding back only enough to pay Miss Fannie Cross; but though they took some time to do the buying, and felt and smoothed everything they bought and put the satin to their cheeks to be sure of its quality, and looked at each other every now and then as if what they were doing was wicked, perhaps, but fearfully enjoyable, still in two days everything was at Miss Fannie's, and it was then I had to be awfully firm with Miss Araminta.

There are some things some women can never take in, and one is that an old sheep should never dress lamb fashion. It was all Miss Fannie (she's a corking-good dressmaker for a small place) and I could do to hold Miss Araminta down when it came to colors, and the cut of her skirt, and some trimmings she wanted to put on the waist. She thinks she loves lavender, but Joseph's coat would have been a colorless piece of apparel beside her dress if we finally hadn't sat on her and told her certain things couldn't be done. She was crazy to pile on a bunch of ancestral lace, yellow and dowdy; but we told her not much, told her freshness and daintiness suited her style much better, and she wasn't old enough to emphasize ances-tral lace, and she blushed and gave in. But nothing would have made her do it if Miss Fannie hadn't thought to throw out the age-line. She caught on and agreed, and after that we did not have a great deal of trouble.

Miss Susanna was a little crankier than I thought she was going to be, and wanted a practical dress that she could wear anywhere at any time, and we had to argue with her a good deal. I told her a train was the thing for her, and I intended to walk behind her the night of the party and keep everybody back far enough to see how grand she looked. When a woman is sixty-six and pretty worn, short skirts for evenings are not impressive, and, though we didn't mention age, we said finally she owed it to her mother's memory to dress in a style suitable to the position into which she had been born, and that settled it. She's the real thing, Miss Susanna is. She doesn't have to play a part.

I had told Miss Fannie on the quiet that the price of making the dresses would be doubled if she would have them ready for the 17th of August, and they were ready. Miss Araminta and Miss Susanna thought it was a bad example to set, as it might not be just to the other Twickenham-Towners to pay more than they could pay, and it stuck Miss Araminta pretty deep to hand out more than was necessary. But I told her it was an emergency operation and that kind always came high. And also I told them that Miss Fannie charged entirely too little for her work, and it was poor religion to go to church on Sunday and sing praises to God and underpay a poor little dressmaker. They said they supposed it was, but I don't think they thought it very reverential in me to speak of God in connection with a dress-maker and what she got for sewing. I gave each one a list of their expenditures, with the cost of everything on it, and each had a little left over after getting their slippers and some sachet powder and a bottle of violet-water apiece, and, after all, that brother of Miss Araminta's got a little of the sapphire money. But it wasn't much. I saw to that. It's been awfully exciting in Twickenham lately.

The event of the year is the MacLean party and the best of everything is saved for it, and in itself it makes every tongue in town talk until you wonder why tongues are the only things that never tire, and then, lo and behold! two days before it came off back comes Elizabeth Hamilton Carter, bringing her beau behind her, and off start the same tongues on a new lap and no breath taken in between.

I wish Billy could see it, the thing Elizabeth brought back! He wears men's clothes (very good ones) and he is twenty-seven years old, and has large hands and feet and ears and a feeble mustache, but as a man he isn't much. He looks like a hatter and is seemingly dumb, and he blinks his eyes so continually that no one can tell their color. Also he bites his finger-nails. I advised Elizabeth to get a beau *pro tem.*, but I didn't mean anything like that. If she wants jealousy to bring Whythe back to her she should keep something on hand to be jealous of. Elizabeth has an iron will and a copper determination, but about as much judgment as a horse-fly.

Miss Bettie Simcoe's eyebrows haven't come down good since the night the *engagées* arrived. She has an explanation for the situation, as she calls it, there never yet being a situation she couldn't explain, and she says the engagement is a piece of management on the part of Elizabeth's aunt on her father's side, the aunt she has been visiting. This aunt is society crazy, and, knowing you can't keep step in society without money, she arranged the whole thing. Anyhow, Elizabeth has a gorgeous ring and a magnificent pin, and of course she ought to be happy if diamonds and things mean happiness, but she isn't happy, and for the first time since I met her I can't make her out. Before I know it I am going to feel sorry for her, and then good-by to in-loveness for me! I have very little sense at times, and no hold-outness at all when certain things come to pass.

Elizabeth still loves Whythe. Engaged or not to some one else, she still cares only for him. I don't want him. I wonder how it might be managed—getting them to take in how silly they have been. I believe I'll try and see if something can't be done. Watchful waiting may be all right in some cases, but I never cared for waiting. Milton says all things come to him who hustles while he waits. You get a move on, Kitty Canary, and see what you can do!

CHAPTER XVIII

The party is over. Everybody who is anybody was at it and we had a perfectly scrumptious time. I never saw so many good things to eat on a hot summer night in all my life, but the heat didn't affect appetites, and Miss Kate Norris, who lives in the Wellington Home (memorial for a dead wife or a live conscience, I don't remember which), ate three platefuls of supper and three helpings of ice-cream. She is fearfully ancestral and an awful eater, and also a sour remarker, and I stay out of her way, but that night I couldn't help seeing the way she made food disappear. No low-born person could have done it quicker.

It was a perfectly beautiful party. The two married daughters of Judge and Mrs. MacLean, who live in the city and always come home for August, were as dear and lovely as if they had never left old Twickenham Town, and their clothes were a liberal education to the stay-at-homers. They were well taken in by the latter, but the sensation of the evening was the arrival and appearance of My Girls, and—oh, my granny!—I was so excited I couldn't stand on both feet at once, and I had to get in a corner and put my back against the wall to keep from making movement. When they came in the room there was a little hush, and then there were so many exclamations of surprise and admiration that I had to fan as hard as Mr. Willie Prince to keep down the blazing red in my face which was there from pride in the dear old darlings and not from heat. And I saw clearer than I had ever seen before that fine things behind one count a good deal, and ancestors of the right kind leave something to their descendants that comes out when needed, and at that party the desirable things came out.

They looked like pictures—Miss Susanna and Miss Araminta— for the prevailing modes, as Miss Araminta calls them, and which she loves so dearly and hits at but never touches, had not been paid very particular attention to, and the thing that suited each had been made for them. They were as becoming to the dresses as the dresses to them. Twickenham nearly lost its breath as they came into the long drawing-room of the MacLean house and walked through it after speaking to the receiving party, and I know now how a mother feels when her debutante daughters are a success. I will have more sympathy with Mother than I used to have, and I will try to behave myself and do the stunts all right for the first year. But she already knows I do not expect to keep on doing them. I have told her.

Nobody can say again that women can't keep a secret, for not even Miss Bettie Simcoe, who knows what the Lord is going to do before He does it, had any idea of the dresses; and though I don't think she or Mrs. General Gaines liked not being told, they were very nice about it and said much kinder things than I thought they were capable of saying. And I really think Elizabeth was pleased also. She actually smiled when she saw her aunt come in with Miss Araminta. Smiles of late have been faint and feeble on the face of the affianced young lady, who isn't playing her part as a person with ancestors ought to play it. She bounced her old beau and took unto herself a new one, and what I can't understand is, having done it, why she doesn't carry it off with a rip-roaring bluff that might fool even herself for a while. But Elizabeth isn't that sort. Everybody is talking about how miserable she looks. I'm afraid I put the beau idea in her head, and the idea has got her in a hole and she doesn't know how to get out of it. I wish Billy was here. He can get a person out of any sort of hole.

I went to the party with Whythe. He has been away for a week, and while away got a new dress suit, which, of course, he wore to the party and looked perfectly grand in it. I think his mother gave the suit to him, though he didn't say, but he was off attending to some business for her, and I'm sure he took it out in the new clothes. It would have been more sensible to have had his teeth fixed, or gotten three new ones, the rest being all right, but it was natural to prefer the suit, and much less painful. Whythe is never going to do anything disagreeable that he can keep from doing.

He was so nice the night of the party that I hadn't the courage to begin finding out the truth or untruth of what Mr. Willie Prince had mentioned as the reason of the rush he had been giving me, and as I don't believe Whythe has ever thought of Father's money, there was no need to be in a hurry to learn whether he had or not. I've had a jolly good time being in love with him, and being made love to, and as an experience it may come in when I begin to write my book. I always did want to know how many ways love can be made in, which, of course, I can never know, for there are as many ways, I guess, as there are men to make it, and the variations on the main theme are as infinitesimal as the tongues that tell the story. It is truly wonderful how differently the same words can be trimmed up and handed out, and I like the crescendoes and diminuendoes and shades of feeling which give emphasis and expression, as my music teacher says I must be careful of when playing. There is never going to be any crescendo or diminuendo business about Billy's love-making, and I might as well make up my mind to that in the beginning. It's going to be pure staccato with him—short and quick and soon over. But it will last forever, Billy's will. He isn't going to stand for foolishness about it when he starts, either. He has two more years at college and then he is going in his father's office.

I don't know what's the matter with Billy. I haven't had a letter from him for a week, or a single card. He must be crazy. I've been so busy I have not written for ten days, and if I don't get a letter soon he won't get one from me for another ten. He can't expect me to do what he doesn't do, and besides, a man doesn't want what he gets too easy, even letters. I don't suppose he could be sick. If he was— I am not going to let myself think sickness or automobile accidents or sliding off mountain peaks (they are in Switzerland now and Billy would get to the top of anything he started for or die trying). And though I say to myself forty times a day he is all right, I wake up at night and wonder if anything could be the matter. I am wondering all the time.

Maybe that is why I was a little nicer to Whythe at the party than I need to have been, because I wanted to forget something it was not well to remember if I was out to enjoy myself. After I had danced with half a dozen boys and spoken to everybody on the place, we went out on the lawn, Whythe and I, and sat on a rustic seat under a great maple-tree to cool off and rest awhile; and though everybody could see us and several couples were under several other trees (a number of cases being on hand and apt to culminate in August), Miss Bettie Simcoe had remarks to make, of course. She made them the next day at breakfast.

I wish I could buy a beau for Miss Bettie and make a present of him to her, but, being a member of the Society for the Prevention of Cruelty to Animals, I couldn't very well do it. I never yet have seen a man I would be that hard on. But it would be the only way she could be made to see some things, and maybe it might make her feel young again. Jess says there's nothing so kittenish as a spinster who's caught an unexpected beau. He is the most rejuvenating thing on earth to a woman who wants one. All don't want them. There are a great many more sensible women in this world than people real- ize, but in certain small places matrimony is still the chief pursuit in which women can engage without being thought unwomanly. Miss Bettie doesn't pursue, and men are good dodgers in this part of the world, but if one of them would say a few things to her of the sort that Whythe knows how to say so well, her sniffing and snorting and seeing might grow less.

I don't like her, but I feel sorry for her, for nobody really loves her, and it must be awful to have nobody to love you best of all on earth. I couldn't live if nobody loved me. I could not. I might live without food and live without drink, and do without clothes and do without air — the right kinds of those things, I mean — but I couldn't and I wouldn't live without loving. As long as I am on this little planet I expect to love a lot of people and I hope they will love me in return. When Miss Bettie makes me so mad I have to go out of the room to keep from saying things I shouldn't, and Miss Araminta simpers so when any one mentions Mr. Sparks's name (he's the new widower minister of the Presbyterian church, with no chance of escape), and Elizabeth Hamilton Carter makes me ashamed of my sex, and I feel like I have swallowed concentrated extract of Human Peculiarities, I remember that not one of them has a father of any sort, much less my sort, or a precious mother and two dandy sisters and a good many nice relations and some bully friends — when I remember all that, remember how many I have to love me, I spit out the peculiarities and try not to mind them, try to see how funny they are. But sometimes the taste sticks right long. I don't suppose I spit right. What I can't understand is that if people want to be loved — and everybody does — why in the name of goodness don't they do a little loving on their own account? You needn't expect to get what you don't give. I'm glad I was born with a taste for liking, though I don't like every one, by a jugful. When I come across a righteous hypocrite I get out of the way, if it isn't convenient to make the hypocrite get out of mine. There are some people I could never congeal with and I am never even going to try.

CHAPTER XIX

I wonder what made me waste time thinking about Miss Bettie Simcoe and human peculiarities when I started to say something about sitting under the trees with Whythe at the MacLean party, but, born a rambler, I will ramble unto death, and there's no use wasting time lamenting natural deficiencies. Whythe, of course, couldn't very conveniently make personal remarks, as people were passing pretty close, though he did say I looked like a dream, which I did not, being too brown for a dream; but I did look real nice. I fished out one of the party dresses Mother made Clarissa put in my trunk, which I haven't worn since I have been here, and I suppose it suited my brownness, as it was creamy and stuck out in the silly way skirts stick now, and it was new-fashioned enough to make everybody look at it and nudge a little. Whythe thought it was lovely, and told me so sixteen times, which was tiresome, and then I saw he was watching Elizabeth, who was on the porch with her new beau and did not know really whether my dress was blue or pink. The only thing he was thinking of was that not far from him was a superseder in possession of something which was once his. Whythe doesn't like to be superseded in anything affecting his personal estimate of himself.

The Lord certainly let loose a lot of contradictions when he started the human race. When I saw the way Whythe was watching Elizabeth, and remembered how she had looked at him when he passed her a few minutes before, I knew two specimens of a common variety were before me, and I made up a parable as I watched them watch each other. The two specimens had been in love and been engaged. They had a fuss. The engagement was broken. She was mad, and he was mad, and each thought the other would make the first advance to own up and make up; but before it could be done a young person appeared and distracted temporarily the attention of the man, and the girl went away to see what she could do. The man repaired the damage done unto him by saying pretty things to the new person, which was good for his pride and kept him in practice, and all was going well when the first maiden returned with a new possession.

The new possession was a son of great wealth, but the Faithless One was made to understand, without words, that his Cruelty was driving the Maid to Marriage with another, and his Vanity was appeased, and in his heart he rejoiced and said unto himself: "It is even as I thought, and that piece of punk she has brought back is bitter unto her, and in comparison to me he is nothingness indeed. And I would arise and punch his head if it were not for the New Person who may love me very much." And the young man was sorrowful when he thought on these things and yet glad also, for the heart of man is receptive to the love of all kinds of women, and it is pleasing unto him to believe he is pleasing unto them.

And seeing that which had come to pass, the New Young Person made up her mind that the Young Man and the Young Maid who had once loved must love again, and in her heart she said it is a vain thing to believe in the words of a man. They cometh out as cometh breath, then pass away and are remembered by him no more. And she took counsel with herself as to how she might bring to pass that which the simple souls knew not how to bring, and, lo! as she thought it came unto her. That's a true parable!

What came was the thought of a picnic. Whythe and Elizabeth must accidentally have a chance to come across each other and have it out, and the best way they could do it would be outdoors, where it is convenient to wander off and get away from nudgers and commenters; and being nothing but impulse, I turned to Whythe, who was still unconsciously watching Elizabeth, and asked him if he would help me with something I was anxious to do. He said of course, and wanted to know what it was. When I told him I would tell him the next day he asked me to drive with him in the morning, and didn't like it because I declined. That is, he didn't like my reason, which was that, as he had been out of his office for some time, his business must need attending to, and I didn't think it ought to be left any longer. He seemed to think that a very unnecessary remark, and I realized he liked Elizabeth's kind better. She would never have dreamed of telling him his business needed attention. Elizabeth is the Admired and Honored type of Womanhood which does not think it is ladylike to have knowledge of business matters.

Seeing the look on his face, I said to myself: "Kitty Canary, it is all over. A pin has been stuck in your balloon and the air is out." And I got up and went in and danced with every man dancer in the room, and hardly knew who they were, the breaks were so often. I had a good time, but also I had a right sinky feeling, for it's pretty wabbly to realize that nothing human is to be depended on very long, and that a girl may be engaged one day to a man and not speaking to him the next. Not that I had ever been engaged. I hadn't, not caring for what goes with engagements, but I might have been if I hadn't remembered about the different things I have fallen in and been fished out of when there was some one by to haul me out. Nobody being by, I had to take care of myself, and I thought it best to go only so far and no farther.

On the way home Whythe tried to say some things pretty low about how he had missed me while away, but Miss Susanna and Miss Araminta were in the back seat of the car (it was Mr. Lipscomb's Ford, and borrowed, of course), and he had to be so careful it was a strain, and as I didn't answer he stopped after a while. It takes two to do more things than make a bargain, and to battledore love without having it shuttlecocked back isn't much fun. He wanted to know what was the matter when I got out, and I told him it was sleep. He didn't seem to like that, either. It's hard to please men.

CHAPTER XX

I didn't see Whythe for the next few days, as I thought it best not to, and, besides, I had bushels of letters to write and a very special one to Father, and I had no time for him. The thing I had to write Father about was money. I wanted five hundred dollars, and the only way I knew how to get it was to ask him to give it to me; so I asked. I always did believe that the person who gives the money ought to be told what is to be done with it, and that is why I wrote Father as I did; and, besides, he likes to hear little bits of news about the Twickenham-Towners, and asking for the money gave me a chance to tell him.

He had told me, when he was here, that if there was any way in which I could be of service in the right way to let him know and he would put up the money part, if I would manage the other part, and it would be a little secret between us and nobody else need know anything about it. When, last week, I heard Mrs. Richard Stafford say she would rather go to a hospital for a month than do anything on earth, I thought my chance had come. At the hospital, she said, a person had the right to be waited on and do nothing, and not think about food or servants, and not feel they were bothering other people by being sick; and while she wasn't sick exactly, a hospital would seem like heaven if she could be in one for a little while. She had laughed when she said it, and didn't dream of its being taken in earnest, but I took it in earnest, for the tiredness in her face makes me ache every time I see her, and right up in my mind popped the little secret Father and I and Miss Polk could have. What I wrote was this:

Father dear, will you please send me five hundred dollars, and if you can do it by return mail I will be very much obliged. The person I want part of it for is so tired that she might not be able to ever get rested unless she has a chance pretty quick to lie down and do nothing for a month, anyhow, and that is why I am in a hurry. Tiredness is a very wearing disease and if it runs on too long it runs a person into a state that is almost impossible to get out of, and the whole family has to pay up for letting it go on. Home gets hell-y when there's too much tiredness in it. What I want the money for is this: Mrs. Stafford is worn out. You know her. She was Miss Mary Shirley, and married a perfectly useless man when she was eighteen, and she is now the mother of seven children, and has a mother-in-law living with her, and also Miss Lou Barbee, who won't go away. And, of course, the man whom she can't turn out. He isn't bad. Just lazy, with nothing to him, but she loves him and I will skip over that part. She needs a rest and ought to have it. It's nothing but scrimp and scrape and strive to keep up appearances day in and day out, year in and year out, until she is all to pieces and the children don't realize what is the matter. And, of course, the Male Person doesn't, for he says that Woman's Place is in the Home. When he told me that yesterday (his heels were on the railing of his porch, where he generally keeps them, and his pipe in his mouth) I thought to myself that if he were mine he would have to get out of my home or prove he had a better right to share it with me than he had ever proved to his wife. But I won't get on that, either. I'll go back to Mrs. Stafford.

Half the time she doesn't have a servant, and all the time she has a mother-in-law, who is pie crust, and Miss Lou Barbee, who's a bagpipe, and with the doors locked and windows shut so no one can see, she has worked herself to death. What I want done is to have an invitation sent her from an old friend to be the guest of the hospital here for a month, and you will be the friend and she will never know it. Miss Polk, the superintendent of the hospital, will manage things. I've talked it over with her, and she understands. Miss Polk is a perfectly grand person. For Simon-pure sense there isn't her equal on earth. She and I have decided on what we would do if we had money. We'd have a Fund for Tired Mothers and Fathers. It would be used to give them a Rest before Death.

I hope you won't mind sending the money. I don't think you will, for everybody says business is so prosperous it's actually unrighteous, and it's in the Bible that you ought to put your treasures where you can find them again, or something like that. If you can't send it I know there will be a good reason for your not sending it, but I would like to have it by Monday if possible, so Mrs. Stafford can go to the Hospital the next day. Later, four other people can have their turn. It is to be used not for illness, but for Tiredness; for broken-downers and worn-outers who need being waited on and fed up and allowed to keep still. Miss Polk and I are going to decide on who needs a rest the most before I go away, and I send you for it, Father dear, an armful of squeezes and the biggest bunch of kisses the mail-man can take.

That was all I told him about the Rest money, but I said a little something about the picnic I thought I ought to give. Everybody in town has given something, and, having accepted, I have to return, and the picnic will be the best thing for Whythe and Elizabeth. I didn't mention the ex-lovers to Father, of course. Even to a father one doesn't have to tell everything in life.

CHAPTER XXI

I haven't seen Whythe alone but once since the night of the Mac-Lean party, and then I stopped any tendencies that showed signs of being personal, and talked most of the time about the picnic which we can't have until late in the month. Every day is engaged up to the twenty-fourth. Whythe tried to talk of Mr. Algernon Grice Baker, but I cut that out also. Sarcasm doesn't suit him, and some day he might be sorry. The Superseder has gone, however, and every day Elizabeth passes Whythe's office, and every day Whythe happens to be at his window at the time of passing. They speak, but so far that is all. I am sorry the picnic has to wait so long. They are two silly children. Their fingers aren't in their mouths, but their heads are on the side when they see each other, and the thing's getting on my nerves. Almost any kind of sin is easier to stand than some sorts of silliness.

I wonder why I stay awake so much at night! It's very unusual, and I try my best to go to sleep, but I can't sleep. Always I am thinking of Mr. William Spencer Sloane and the things I would say to him if he were in hearing distance. Not one line have I had from him for more than two weeks. Not a card or a little present, which he usually sends from every place he goes to, or any sign to show he is living. I got so mad when I realized he hadn't noticed me for fourteen days that I couldn't keep in things which had to come out, and, seeing Miss Susanna was sleeping the sleep of worn-outness, I got up the other night and lighted a candle behind the bed, and on the floor I wrote a letter that maybe wasn't altogether as accurate as it might have been. I wouldn't have sent it the next day if it hadn't been for a letter I got from Jess, but after I read hers I sent mine flying.

I haven't cooled down yet from reading Jess's letter. I am not going to cool down until I see the cause of it face to face, and if Billy thinks it makes the least difference to me how he amuses himself or with whom he spends his time sightseeing he thinks Wrong! I was going to tear up the letter I had written him in the middle of the night for the relief of indignations and because in the middle of the night things seem so much bigger and harder and stranger than in the daylight; but after I read the letter from Jess I added a postscript to mine and almost ran down to the post-office to mail it, for fear if I didn't do it quick I mightn't do it at all. Ever since I sent it off I have been perfectly horrid, and I can hardly stand myself. I have put off trying to make Whythe and Elizabeth see how stupid they are, and as Elizabeth hasn't been very nice to me I haven't felt it to be my duty to show her what a goose she is. Neither have I told Whythe that almost any girl who adored him would do for his wife. As I don't adore I wouldn't do, and I think he is beginning to take it in. A dozen times of late he has told me he doesn't understand me. He does not. And never will.

The thing in Jess's letter which made me hot was this: "What is the matter with you and Billy? Pat says (Pat is Patricia, Billy's sister) that you've been pretty horrid about writing him, and he's been blue-black at not getting letters from you; but at present he is having a good time with a very jolly girl from the West who is at their hotel. Chirp him something cheerful, Canary Bird. If I were younger or Billy older you shouldn't have him. I'd have him myself. I'm not going to stand for bad treatment of him, and if those Southern boys who make love to every pretty girl they see, and make it better than any boys on earth, have made you forget an old friend, I'm coming down and take you back home. Behave yourself, Kitty Canary, and write Billy the sort of letter we scream over up here." And then she went on with other things.

It is ridiculous in Pat to say I haven't written Billy! I have. Three long letters and three cards, and certainly he can't expect more than that, as he hasn't been gone but two months and five days; and, besides, friends ought to have such confidence in each other that they don't need letters to prove their friendship. Not a word have I had from him in more than two weeks, and if Jess thinks I am going to write him a chirp letter (which he won't have time to read if he is going around so much with a Western girl and having so much fun) she, too, thinks Wrong. That Westerner explains why I haven't heard from him for so long. It is outrageous in Billy to behave as he has been behaving. All men are alike. Every one of them. It was ignorance in me to imagine Billy was different. He isn't. The more I thought of how mistaken I had been in him the madder I got, and I just wrote a postscript to my letter and flew to the post-office with it. It seemed providential that my letter was ready to send. I hope he will read it while on one of his joyous excursions with the Western Woman, who is doubtless twenty-five, maybe thirty, and just making use of Billy, who hasn't sense enough to see it. I nearly cried my eyes out last night, before Miss Susanna came up to bed, because it was necessary to send him such a letter. Still, Billy has to learn things in life and he might as well learn them early. What I wrote was this:

Dear Billy, — I have been having such a perfectly grand time lately that it has been impossible to squeeze out a scrap in which to write you, and yet I have wanted to do so, for I am sure you will be glad to know how fearfully happy I am and what is causing the happiness. I am in love. It is the most wonderful thing I have ever been in, and thrillingly interesting. I suppose

you have been in it many times, but not my way, or you would have men-
tioned it, just as I am doing to you, as we are such old friends, and friends
have the right to know of important happenings. I hope you will like each
other when you meet, for, though you are very unlike, you are both made of
male material, and I have often noticed that men have many peculiarities in
common. One of them is out of sight out of love, and a great readiness to be
admired and entertained. He is a lawyer and couldn't be better born,
though he might be better educated; still, one mustn't expect all things in
one man, and his eyes are so wonderful, and he uses such poetic prose, that
the lack of money and a few other lacks shouldn't count. He lives in a beau-
tiful old house which has proud traditions and no bathrooms, and his fami-
ly is one of the oldest and most disagreeable in America; still, we would not
have to live with them if we were married. Nothing on earth could make me
sleep under the same roof with his sisters, who are so churchy that the
minister himself is subject under them. And neither would it be safe for me
to be too closely associated with his mother. However, things of that sort
are in the distance, which may be far or may not, and I am not thinking of
immediate marriage, but just how magnificent it is to have somebody in
love with you who knows how to say so in the most delicious way, and
with a voice that, when the moon is out, is truly heavenly. I am telling you
about it because I thought you might be interested and would like to know
of my happiness; but, of course, I don't want you to tell any one else, as it
is still a secret and all so indefinite that it wouldn't do to speak of it to any
one but you. I am scribbling this in the middle of the night, because I can't
sleep for thinking of some one, and because there is no time in the day in
which to write. I hope you are having a great time. Give my love to the
family and write me of your gladness at knowing of mine.

As ever,
   Kitty.

Now what do you suppose made me write such slush as that?
And why is a female person born with such horridness in her that
she can say things that are not so with a smile in public and cry her
eyes out when alone? That's what I have been doing lately, though I
can't let tears have much time, for I am not by nature a crier, and
they would disturb Miss Susanna at night. In my secret heart I just
wrote that letter to Billy because I was indignant with him for not
writing to me for more than two weeks, and I didn't intend to let

him think I was sitting on a tombstone waving a willow branch in one hand and wiping tears away with the other. And, besides, I have been in love. Summer love. And it has been exciting. No one could expect me to go through life and not have but one experience in love making and hearing, and because a girl enjoys the different manners of expression it doesn't mean she is not particular about the story not being illustrated. I don't illustrate or allow illustrations, which, of course, lessens some of the thrill, but I promised Jess I would always draw the line at the right time, and I have. I have not been engaged for half a minute, and I wouldn't have added the postscript if it hadn't been for her letter and what she told me about that girl from some Western town who is no more his sort than I am her brother's. Billy is perfectly blind about some things, and has no discrimination where it is most needed. Anyhow, I added the postscript:

P.S. — By the time you get this I may be engaged. Thank you for what you would say if here.

K. C.

CHAPTER XXII

It was after I sent the letter that I got so restless I couldn't sit still, and as there was nothing I enjoyed doing I spent a good deal of my tune at the hospital with Miss Polk, who is a very splendid person, and every day I went in to see Mrs. Stafford. She is having the grandest rest, with rubs and good eats and nothing to do but be waited on and cared for, that a tired person ever had, and I am the only one who is allowed to see her, which is beyond the understanding of Twickenham Town. I'm cheerful is the reason I'm allowed to see her, the town is told, and that's enough for it to know.

It certainly is queer how some things happen in the nick of time. Father sent me the money, but told me to try to be as practical as possible, knowing I am given to doing impractical things; and I took it to Miss Polk, and nobody but she and I know where it came from.

And then she invited Mrs. Stafford to be a guest of the hospital for a month. I happened to be at the house when the note came. I thought it best to be there accidentally, in case there should be argument and talk, and the Man of the House should still think Woman's Place was in the Home, and sure enough there was. Mrs. Stafford read the note, and her face got as white as death, and after a minute she said it would be heaven to go, but of course she couldn't. And the noble creature who is her husband said it was very presumptuous in whoever had invited her to be the guest of the hospital, and that he wasn't in the habit of having his wife visit such places on the invitation of unknown interferers, and of course she couldn't go. And just as he said that Mrs. Stafford keeled over in a dead faint right at his feet, as if something had given out at the thought of rest. I knew that was my chance, and I took it.

"Stop that automobile!" I waved to a man who was coming down the street, and as he stopped I knelt and did the things Billy had made me learn how to do the first year we went to camp. And seeing the poor, tired soul had just fainted, and would come to in a minute, I spoke quick to the man looking down at her, scared to death, as were the children, who began to cry, and told him he wouldn't have a wife much longer to be interfered with if he didn't come down from that horse he thought he was riding and have some common sense.

"Don't you see she is worn out," I said, "and got nothing to go on with? Everything has given out, and the next time she drops over in this way she may never get up again." I was putting some water on her face as I spoke, and, seeing her eyes begin to open a little, I called to Mr. Everett, who had gotten out of his car and was on the porch, to help Mr. Stafford put his wife in and take her to the hospital, and the frightened husband for once did as he was told. I hopped in with her and held her up and told Mr. Everett to drive like old Scratch, and he drove. It was all over so quickly nobody knew what had happened.

It was like somebody being kidnapped and dragged off by highwaymen, taking her away so hurriedly, but if it hadn't been done that way there would have been endless talk and a thousand reasons why she couldn't go; and if she hadn't she would have soon gone for good. Sometimes somebody has to be high-handed, and even if that billy-goat of a husband pretends to resent what I did his wife isn't resenting it, and she is the one that counts. I always agree with her that it was such a strange thing I happened to be there the day the note came. And also she thinks it strange I decided so quickly to take her to the hospital, when she had just said she couldn't go. I tell her I do a good many things on the spur of the moment, and getting the men to pick her up and hurry away with her was just another case of spur, and she shuts her eyes when I say that and looks as if she is praying. The lucky part was her fainting at the right time. Anyhow, she is at the hospital, and that old rooster of hers is finding out a good many things it took her absence from home for him to learn. I never expect to get married. NEVER!

CHAPTER XXIII

I have just found out why Elizabeth and Whythe had their break. Miss Bettie Simcoe told me. It took Miss Bettie some time to get at the bottom of it, but Elizabeth told her last night, and this morning I was given the information at the first moment Miss Bettie could get me to herself.

Elizabeth was dead right in the stand she took, but her little spurt of independence didn't last long, and she is now ready to give in when the chance comes to give. Miss Bettie added that on her own account. Whythe couldn't afford to be married, but that wasn't to interfere with his marriage. He had expected to take Elizabeth to his mother's home and plant her in it, but when he told her Elizabeth balked. She preferred to stay with her aunt Susanna after her marriage to going to Whythe's home, and when she so informed him he said things he shouldn't, and then both sent off skyrockets and the whole thing went up in the air. And then I came.

She has now changed her mind and is willing to follow her husband wherever he leads. She is truly womanly, also she is still wearing the ring of the beau with whom she sought to bring Whythe to terms, and to please her worldly aunt. But she will return the ring when it is proper to do so. She is waiting to find out.

Elizabeth had more sense than I gave her credit for in refusing to live in the House of Eppes; but it's either live there or not live with Whythe, and she evidently can't live without him. I'd hate love to make me lose the little gumption I was born with, and even my little knows no house is big enough for a son's wife and a mother-in-law and three in-law sisters. It won't be a Home, Sweet Home, place when Elizabeth enters the Eppes house, and it will be nip and tuck as to who wins out, but that's not my business. I'm sorry for both sides, and thankful I'm not related to either. Also, I will get out of the way as soon as possible, but until the picnic there doesn't seem a possible way.

There is nothing in life that is not over if life is long enough, and my little love affair with Mr. Whythe Rives Eppes belongs to the past. Elizabeth can have him any minute she wants, and unless actions do not speak louder than words she wants him right away, and he her. I do not see how she is possibly going to stand his teeth. Still, there are a great many things I do not understand in life.

The picnic is over. By giving it I brought down a good deal of comment and criticism on my brown and curly head, but it does not matter. Nothing except sin really matters if we have sense enough to see it. I invited everybody in Twickenham Town that I liked to the picnic, and some few I didn't, the latter being relations of those I did. I don't think a person ought to be punished for their relations, any more than being held responsible for them, and so I included them, too. What I was criticized for was asking to the picnic quite a number of people who don't usually go to the same places at the same time the Historicals go, and it made talk. That night Miss Araminta Armstrong, on the quiet, told me she knew I meant to do right, but one had to use judgment in life, and it wasn't well to put ideas in some people's heads. I told her I knew it, knew certain kinds of heads couldn't take in certain ideas, one of which was that people could enjoy friendliness and outdoorness and a lunch they didn't have to prepare for themselves, even if they were not high-born, and as the ones referred to did not have contagious diseases their presence wouldn't prove dangerous and the Ancestrals needn't be uneasy. Also I told her I didn't care for judgment as much as I ought, and if human beings knew one another better they might find they were not as unlike as they thought. She didn't say anything more. Neither did any one else say anything to me. To one another they said a good deal.

It was at the picnic I had a little talk with Whythe. We went down to a stream under a big willow-tree, and he started on the usual, but I told him he must not say anything more to me on that subject, and if he were the man I thought him he would not allow Elizabeth to marry the Compensator she was no more in love with than I was. Also, I said a few more things that were pleasant for him to hear, such as Elizabeth's heart was breaking (it was, as much as her kind of heart could break), and I told him it was foolishness to ruin one's life because of a misunderstanding, and that both had doubtless been in the wrong. And incidentally I let drop that if, after years of preparation, I ever got married I would have nothing to bring my husband but myself, as my father had made up his mind that young people should make their own way in life (he ought to have so made it up if he hasn't), and Whythe said that cut no figure with him, and asked me point-blank if I did not love him. It didn't sound polite to say no, and yet I couldn't truthfully say yes, so I just sighed and shook my head. When he asked me if I could give him no hope, I answered *no* with such uncomplimentary quickness that I had to cough to overcome it, and then I told him it was impossible for a girl of Elizabeth's taste and training and character, who had once loved such a man as he, to really care for any one else. And the blackness in his face, caused by my unnecessary emphasis, died out, and I saw he was agreeing with me concerning Elizabeth, and that I would not have to insist on what I said being so. A man's appetite for flattery is never poor, and usually it is hearty. When we got up to go back to where lunch was being served Whythe had quite a determined air about him. I told him if I could help in any way to let me know. An hour later I saw him and Elizabeth going down to the same stream and the same old willow tree.

When the time came to go home I pretended I had to see Florence Kensey about something that was important, and in the confusion of getting the people in the cars I managed to have Whythe put Elizabeth in his, and told them to get away quick and I would come on with Mason Page. They got. And the next day Elizabeth looked like some one who had been unbandaged and was letting out breath that for a long time had been held in. Also, she looked pinker and whiter than ever, and so Pure that it was not possible for me to stay close to her, so I got away. No longer Hurt and Misunderstood, she went about smiling in sweet triumphantness that was not put in words, but oozed without them, and her manner to me was one of deepest sympathy. Poor Whythe!

CHAPTER XXIV

There are some things not required of human nature to stand. Elizabeth Hamilton Carter is one of them. I was glad to give her back her beau. I felt truly Virginian in doing it, for Virginians always say, when giving you something, that they don't want it; I certainly didn't want Whythe. I wouldn't have known what to do with him after the summer was over, and I was conscious of great relief in getting him off my hands without further loss or trouble. I couldn't tell Elizabeth this, of course, though there were times when it took a good deal of something I did not know I had to keep from doing so. Also, it took more strength to keep several other things to myself than I knew I possessed. It took praying and the end of the sheet to do it, but I did it, and I'm getting encouraged about K. C.

What encourages me is this: Two nights after the picnic Elizabeth came to my room and asked if she might have a little talk with me, as she felt she ought to. I told her she could, and she sat down and began. Miss Susanna was back in her own quarters, the people from Florida having gone, and I had just finished saying my prayers and was ready to hop into bed when Elizabeth knocked at my door. I knew what was coming from the look on her face and her manner of walking, and the way she held her head.

If ever I write that book I am always thinking about I am going to put Elizabeth in it as well as Miss Araminta Armstrong, and if I could get some men to match them I would have some corking characters to begin with. But no kind of pen-and-ink picture of Elizabeth would do her justice. Her sweetness of speech when she is particularly nasty is beyond the power of human portrayal. I got in bed quick when she said she wanted to talk, because I was afraid I might have to hit something, and the pillow was the only thing I could manage without sound. I put it where I could give it a dig when politeness required control, and told her to go ahead.

In her last sleep Elizabeth will pose. She took her seat near the window where the moonlight could shine on her (she looked very pretty in her pink-silk kimono, a hand-over from her rich aunt, and shabby but becoming in color), and for a moment she didn't say anything, just fooled with the pink ribbon on her hair. And then she said she had a secret to tell me; said it so soft, with her head on the side, that I had to ask her to speak louder please, and I got nearer the edge of the bed. Elbow on it and chin in the palm of one hand, I prayed hard to be polite in my own room, and reached out for an end of the sheet with the other. Again I told her to go ahead. After a minute she went.

"You and Whythe have been such friends that I think you should be the first to know that—"

"Have you and Whythe made up?" I stuck my bare foot over the edge of the bed and wriggled it. "If you have you had better be married quick and not take any more chances. I'm awfully glad if things are settled. Have you bounced the other fellow yet?"

It was cruel in me to take out of her mouth what she was moistening her lips to say, but I was sleepy and I didn't want details. She had no idea of being cut out of saying what it was her determination to say, however, considering I had been responsible for some unhappy days during the past two months, and before she got through she had said all she wanted me to hear. If it hadn't been for the pillow I would have rolled out of bed. The nerve of her! The belief of her! And, oh, my granny! the punishment, as she imagined, of me!

Before she left the room she told me she could no longer hold out against Whythe's pleadings. Told me he had suffered so during the summer she was uneasy about him, and, though he had tried to forget, it had been useless, and, unable to endure it any longer, he had come to her and told her he could stand no more, and if she did not promise to marry him at once he would—he would— Her voice trailed, but I said nothing, the end of the sheet being stuffed into my mouth for politeness' sake, and when her tears had been wiped away she began again.

"It is hard to forgive Whythe, because you are so young, and he knows how fascinating he is and how little experience you have had with young men, but his father was a flirt before him" (poor Father! I thought of the retribution that had come to him in Mother, and I pushed in more sheet), "and it is natural in a man to seek amusement and entertainment when he is suffering as Whythe was. I hope you will forgive him. It is because he may have made you imagine things that were not so, and because you have been so nice to him, that I thought you should be the first to know."

I rolled back to the side of the bed facing her, from which I had rolled the other way for safety, and took the end of the sheet out of my mouth. "Have you told IT?" I asked. "It doesn't make any difference about my knowing as I knew before you did, but something is due that which you brought back with you. Have you told IT, Elizabeth?"

"Told who? I don't understand." She sat up. "I don't know who you are talking about."

"Don't you?" I too sat up and swung my bare feet over the side of the bed. "I am talking about the person to whom I read in the Twickenham Town Sentinel that you were engaged. He dresses like a man, and he may be one, but even if he isn't he deserves to be treated decently by the lady who had promised to marry him. I suppose he knows." I nodded to her hand, on which was the ring he had given her and which she had been twirling as she talked. "That is, if you have had time to tell him."

"That is entirely my affair!" When not hurt or injured Elizabeth is superior, and she added scorn to the tone of her voice, but stopped fooling with the ring, which I know she hated to send back. "I see you do not appreciate the confidence I am putting in you or the compliment I am paying you by telling you first, and if that is the case I will go." She made movement as if to get up, but she had no idea of going, so I didn't notice it, but kept on swinging my feet, and then I asked her if she had told Miss Susanna, and if she hadn't she ought to at once, Miss Susanna being closely related and I nothing but a summer boarder. And I said I hoped she would be married right away, as I would love to be at the wedding, and if she would ask me to be one of the bridesmaids I would be one with pleasure. But she wouldn't answer me. Seeing she still had something to say, and wouldn't leave until she said it, I put my feet back in bed and lay flat with my hands under my head and my eyes shut, and when at last I was fixed and quiet she began for a third time.

I don't remember a thing after that except a sort of monotone voice and something about people talking about me because I had accepted Whythe's attentions when everybody knew—I didn't hear what everybody knew, and not until I did hear a sound at the door did I wake up good, and then I jumped as if shot and asked her, half-asleep, if she were going to live with Mother and Sister and Sister Edwina and Miss Lily Lou when she was married, but she answered not. And since her midnight confession she hath not opened her mouth unto me and her little lips get together when she sees me coming, and from her friends I have learned that she is deeply distressed at my treatment of her. And to her friends I have said Rats! and so endeth the efforts at friendship which she imagined she had made. I am never going to pretend to be friends with a person who is not truthful, and whom I understand as I understand Elizabeth Hamilton Carter. I don't like her, and though it is not necessary to say so unless occasion requires, neither is it necessary to appear to be what I am not. I like Whythe, and when I saw him a few days after Elizabeth gave herself the satisfaction of communicating to me the return of his tempted affections, I shook hands with him good and hard and wished him all the happiness I knew there was little chance of his getting. If I were a man and had to live in the house with a female who shut her mouth tight every time she got mad and was continually hurt and always sensitive, there would likely be in that house battle, murder, or sudden death. Any kind of outspokenness is better to be endured than silent offense.

CHAPTER XXV

This is the last day of August, and it is a day Twickenham Town is going to remember for a long time. I have done again that which I should not have done, and I guess I had better go home. I had expected to stay until the twenty-seventh of September and return with Father, who was to spend a week here with me, but he can't come.

I suppose it was the awful disappointment of knowing Father couldn't come, and being so miserable myself (not one line yet from that person named William Spencer Sloane, who is probably married to an elderly woman by this time), and because of my sureness that no human being could be depended on in time of temptation, especially vigorous, aggressive temptations that come out of the West, that I gave help where help seemed to be needed, and now again I am in everybody's mouth. Also my ankles are still a little sore from the weight of the window being on them as I hung out, but they are nearly well, and even if they were not it would not matter. Two young hearts are happy and a proud person is not, and the blame is on me. That also doesn't matter. I am soon going away.

The thing I did, which maybe I shouldn't have done, was to help little Amy Frances Winston get married. She is the property of her grandmother, who is a very important part of Twickenham Town. Having no parents or sisters or brothers, and only enough money of her own for her keep, and no spunk or spirit, she has gone on for years loving an awfully nice chap named Taylor French, with little chance of ever marrying him, and then in hops this Miss Frisk, who asks her why she doesn't quit fumbling and stop fearing, and the thing is done.

There is nothing the matter with Taylor French except he is not Ancestral. Mrs. Brandon, Amy's grandmother, is diseased on the subject of ancestry, and the first thing she asks about a man is who is he. Knowing she would want to know who I was, I mentioned to her one day that I had never had any grandparents on either side (living ones I meant), and that we were not historic, and no member of our family had ever been distinguished (for righteousness, though I didn't use the word), and that we had made our own way in life, which was true, for Father didn't have a thing but what he was making when he married Mother. I also told her I did not mind in the least, and if I did I would try to remember that Christ was a carpenter and St. Paul a sail-maker, though I'd never care to be intimate with St. Paul. And I told her I thought it was yourself that counted most, after all, and not dead people, though it must be nice to know somebody in your family had been something if you were not. All she said was, "Are you a suffragist?" When I said I was and I hoped I didn't look as if I were not, for I wouldn't like anybody to be mistaken about it, she gave me a long look and left the room.

She did not exactly draw her skirts aside with her hand as she passed me, but she did it inwardly; that is, I imagined she did from the expression of her face, and the next day she must have fumigated the house, for when I went by an awful smell of sulphur was coming from it. She is a low bender and bower in church at the mention of a name belonging to one she believes a Prince in disguise, who in another life will receive her into His kingdom, and whom she professes to follow in the expectation of being rewarded for so doing, but her head is held high when she doesn't care to see the lowly ones He came to give light and life to. I don't mean she doesn't give old clothes and food and sometimes a little wood to old Mrs. Snicker, who can't move, from rheumatism, but she would no more speak other than stiffly to some of the people I know here than she would go in for suffrage. She doesn't realize she is a living woman. She thinks she is an Ancestor. For years she has forbidden Taylor French to come to her house, and Amy has to see him elsewhere.

She has seen a good deal of him lately, Amy has. Taylor doesn't live in Twickenham Town now. He is living in North Carolina and has a good position, and is able to get married (I know because I asked him), and any minute day or night in the past eighteen months in which Amy would have agreed he would have married her and taken her away, but Amy wouldn't agree. Things have been dragging along this way so long that the nerves of both are frazzled out, and there's nothing to hope for but death, and, of course, it isn't respectful to think too hopefully of death and a grandmother. And then I popped in and gave things a little push and the curtain dropped.

The way it dropped was this. I mean the way they got married. Taylor was in town the last two weeks in August, and, as everybody invited him to their parties, he and Amy managed to see a good deal of each other (also the seeing wasn't altogether at places where other people were around). But she wasn't allowed to meet him on the square or to receive letters from him straight. And sometimes, if he wanted to say something in a hurry, or send her candy or a new book, or any of the usuals, he had to give a signal by throwing pebbles on her window at night, and then she would throw out a string and he would tie the thing to it and she would haul up, and the Personage, who was usually asleep, would be none the wiser. The Personage is deaf, which is a great help.

Well, one night three of the town girls and myself, with a boy apiece, had been to see Amy, and when we went up-stairs (just the girls) to see a new hat a city cousin had sent her, we heard a little tap at the west window. It had been raining, which accounted for our being indoors with the windows lowered, and when we heard the tapping we were so excited we could hardly breathe. It was fearfully thrilly, just like things one reads about in books, and I told the girls to put out the light quick, and when it was out I went to the window and saw Taylor standing in the shadow of a big tree. He signaled me to drop the line, but when I threw the piece of twine Amy gave me I threw it wrong and it got caught in a broken piece of shingle on the edge of the porch and hung there. I couldn't get it back and Taylor couldn't get it down, and, seeing it was necessary for something to be done, I pushed aside the curtains (they were made of striped calico, blue and white) and told the girls I was going to lean out of the window on the roof of the porch to get the string loose, and they must hold on to my feet, for the roof sloped and I might slip if they didn't. They tried to stop me, and Amy wrung her hands, being very nervous from living on a strain and loving in secret, but I was out head foremost in a jiffy, and all four made a grab for my feet and legs. Being flat on my stomach, and having long arms, I got the string off from the piece of shingle, and just as I did it and threw it to Taylor I heard a noise and a little cry from the girls, something about, "Oh, my goodness! here she comes!" and I knew what had happened.

"Pull the window down on my feet and let go," I called, as loud as I dared, "and draw the curtains so she won't see my shoes. If she asks where I am, tell her I am outdoors. Quick! Let it down!"

They got it down and drew the curtains just as her Royal Highness walked in, and as she went toward the window Katherine
Hardy says that never before had she prayed as she prayed that
minute, and then she thought of mice, which was a quick answer.
She gave a little scream and jumped with her hands over her eyes
and bumped into the lady, who, being a woman first, was also
afraid of mice, and she moved, too. Seeing the girls flying around,
she told them to stop, told them Maud Hendren's mother had telephoned that she must come home at once and, not missing me,
owing to the girls moving about so she wouldn't notice, she went
out of the room, skirts still held up, and the minute she was out they
rushed for the window and pulled me in.

My dress was a sight when I got in, and I didn't have much skin
on my elbows, and my hands were stuck up with splinters, as I had
to hold on to anything I could clutch, being afraid the window
would not hold my feet and the shingles being rotten. But otherwise
no damage was done, and I got the note Taylor had tied to the
string, which I had pulled up by the time the Ogress had departed. I
gave it to Amy and told her to read it quick.

She read it, and after doing it turned so white and looked so
queer we were frightened. For a minute she couldn't speak, then she
handed me the note, and when I asked if I must read it aloud she
nodded her head and sat down, as if to stand up was impossible. I
glanced over it first so as to leave out the little love decorations and
just read the practical part, and what Taylor told her was that he
had just gotten a telegram from his house (it's iron-works I think)
saying he must leave on important business for South America on
the 6th of September. The house had been talking of sending him
for some time, and had been waiting for certain developments
which had suddenly developed, and he would have to go. Would
she go with him, and if she would not he never expected to come
back again, but would stay over there and take charge of the South-
American branch of the house he was going to establish. She would
have to decide at once, as he couldn't stay a minute later than the
30th. They could be married anywhere she said, only it must be
quickly done. He had gotten the telegram an hour before, and in the
morning she must get Kitty Canary to fix things so he could see her
and talk more fully. Kitty could be depended on and would manage

somehow. The rest being private and personal, I skipped it and gave the note back to Amy, who was as white as the dress she had on, and her hands as limp as wet kid gloves.

Excited! To my dying day I will never forget the thrill of it. Being in love myself, as I had once thought, wasn't a circumstance to it, and the other girls were as bad as I. To help a heart-yearning, back-boneless young girl escape from the captivity of a cast-iron grand-parent was something no red-blooded person could refuse, and every one of us agreed that the only thing for Amy to do was to walk into the den of lions and tell the head lioness the truth; ask her permission to many the man she loved, and, if she would not give it, to take it, anyhow, and tell her farewell and leave at once for South America. That, at least, was what I thought ought to be done, and after a while the others thought so, too. At first there was a lot of argument, but I told them I would never agree to Amy's running away to be married without her first telling her grandmother she was going to do it. That is, if she would not let her be married at home. If the G. M. would not let, then Amy could take the first train out, but she mustn't take it until she had shown her grandmother the respect she did not deserve. I never could bear runaway mar-riages. There's always something so common about them, and I wasn't going to be party to one if I could help it.

All the time we were talking we left Amy out of it, and never once asked her what she preferred in the matter. The reason we didn't was the poor little thing was so frightened and distressed that she could not open her lips. We would not let her come down-stairs with us, and when we said good night I whispered that I would see Taylor on my way to Rose Hill, and at ten o'clock the next morning we would meet her at the back of Miss Susanna's vegetable garden under the big locust-tree, and that she mustn't worry, we'd fix it, he and I. Also I told her she might bring up some toilet things and little traveling necessities and leave them with me; and though she clung to me like a frightened child and didn't speak, she was down by the barn the next morning at ten, and so was Taylor. I let them get there a little ahead of me.

CHAPTER XXVI

They are married and gone, and for two days Twickenham Town has talked of nothing else. It made a regular soup of the marriage. The bride and groom were the stock, the grandparent and maiden aunts were the thickening, and I was the seasoning; but all that does not matter now. The ancestralized person has learned that the twentieth century sees some things clearer than the eighteenth did, but she will never admit that she has learned it. Taylor and Amy were not unmindful of what was due her, however. Taylor wrote her a very nice letter, asking her permission to marry her granddaughter and take her to South America, and her answer was low-down. He wrote as a gentleman should, and she answered as a lady shouldn't, for her answer was insulting, and a real lady never humiliates any one. After reading it Taylor told Amy to meet him at seven o'clock on Wednesday morning, and they would be married in the church with no one present but his brother (the only relative Taylor has in town is a bachelor brother), and the sexton, the minister, and me. She met and the marriage took place.

We didn't tell a soul about the marriage. The night before Amy spent with me at Rose Hill, and, thinking it best Taylor should not be there, I told him not to come, and sent the other boys home early. In my room I packed my suitcase and put in it two dresses I had never worn, which I was glad to do, as it would mean that much less to pack when I went home, and also I put in some other things; and though Amy cried a good deal and didn't think she ought to take them, she was very particular about how they went in. She is very neat and careful, and I'm fearfully quick, so it was well she watched me. I told her she was doing me a favor to dispossess me of what I didn't want and what was in my way, and as we were the same height, though Amy is a little thinner, owing to secret love and distress of mind, I knew the things would fit her, and I was more than glad to get rid of them. Also she didn't have any of her own convenient, and she might as well be sensible. She was, and put in her own tooth brush and powder and left the rest to me, and by eleven o'clock everything was ready.

When the next day the news flew around that the marriage had taken place and I had been the leading spirit in it, I went to bed and stayed there until the town had finished chewing me up, and then I came out again. It was the most sensible thing I ever did and saved a lot of talk and argument.

Another reason I went to bed was because I was so homesick and so lonely, and so something I had no name for, that I knew it was wiser to be by myself. I can't be much in life, but I can keep from being a nuisance, and when you feel you haven't a friend on earth outside of your family, who sometimes are queer also, you're apt to be a trial to those you come in contact with. For two whole days I stayed in my room and thought of nothing but a big, brawny, domineering, dictating girl from the West who was giving Billy no time to write letters; and though I would die before I would let anybody know it, even Jess, I nearly cried my eyes out under the bedclothes the day of the marriage.

Life is a poor thing at times. And it is never so poor as when you think a friend has failed you. There was nothing on earth that could have made me believe Billy would ever fail me when we had known each other since children, and he had saved my life three or four times; but how can I help believing it when he is letting a perfectly ordinary, straight-haired, large-footed girl from the West make him forget that I am living and spending the summer in Twickenham Town? If he had not forgotten, would he not write? He would. I am miserable and I will never be happy until I can say some things to William Spencer Sloane that he ought to hear. But I'm trying to keep my miserableness to myself. People aren't interested in other people's miseries. I wonder if I will ever again get a letter from Billy!

CHAPTER XXVII

It is a perfectly magnificent thing to be alive! And this world is a perfectly glorious place to be alive in! There isn't a bird in Twickenham Town that isn't singing to-day, or a flower that isn't blooming, and, owing to the rain last night, the dust is laying. As for the sun—there couldn't be a more shining one, and the sky is a blue so gorgeous that it seems heaven turned inside out, and in the air is the snap of coolness that makes one want to walk and walk and walk, and its crispness means fall is coming. I love the fall. I can't think of anything I do not love to-day except Elizabeth Hamilton Carter and Grandmother Brandon, and I don't exactly abhor them. I just don't like them, and prefer to stay out of their way. But everybody else in town is a dear, and I wish I knew I was coming back next summer. That is—

It doesn't matter what is or what isn't. The thing that matters is that this morning I went to the post-office, as usual, but, what was not as usual, I got what I had long been looking for, and which had come not for endless, endless days. When I saw the big batch of letters and things from Billy, and knew that all my fears were at an end, I was so excited I could not speak without signs that shouldn't show, and, lest some one stop me, I put the mail inside my shirt-waist and hopped on Skylark and flew out of town.

I didn't stop until I got to a big chestnut-tree about three miles from Rose Hill, and there I took off Skylark's bridle and let her have all the grass she could eat, and then I sat down and sorted the letters out. There were four from Billy and twelve cards and two packages, and at first I couldn't understand why they had been held up, why I hadn't gotten them before; and then I saw they were postmarked from the same place, and had been mailed within three days of one another. That puzzled me, so I decided to open them and find out what was the matter—whether it was the Western girl or something else.

I ought to have known it was something else! And I have been wondering, ever since I read the letters and found out about the accident to Billy's eyes, when he came near being shot and the powder got in them and nearly put them out, why it is that people are so mistrusting and why we let one thing we can't understand make us forget what we ought to understand very well. Ten thousand kind things, right things, nice things we take for granted, and then at the first thing we think isn't kind or right or nice we forget the others and howl and snort about the one we do not like. At least that is what I did. Not outwardly, of course, but inwardly, for I'm pretty toplofty about being treated right, and I flare out and say things I shouldn't at times, and afterward I am so ashamed of myself that a worm of the dust is a perky animal to me for a few minutes. That condition of mind doesn't last very long, however. I am not by nature a humble-minded person. While it does last it is awful. Perfectly awful.

When I read Billy's letter I laid right down on the grass and put my face deep down in it, and there wasn't anything abominable that anybody could have said about me that I would not have agreed to. All the time I had been furious with him for not writing as usual, he had been shut up in a dark room, not able to see the food he was eating, much less able to write letters, and then when they took the bandages off he wrote so much they had to be put back again, and he was forbidden to write more than a few lines, which accounted for so many cards. He wouldn't let any one else write me, and I don't understand exactly how it happened except he saw a drunken man on the street waving a pistol, and there were some children around, and before the policeman could get to him Billy had caught his hand and the thing had gone off and some of the powder got in his eyes. He made light of it, but I know exactly what he did. I thought it was a Western product that was engrossing him, and it was the children he was trying to save. Oh, Billy, I'm a pig! A perfectly horrid pig!

And then I suddenly thought of the astonishing letter I had written about being in love and maybe engaged, and I prayed hard that he would never get it; but I knew it was too late for prayers. And then I got mad with Pat for writing to Jess about the girl from the West, and with Jess for writing what Pat had written, and not for some time did I come to my senses and realize I was the only person I had any right to get mad with. I got, all right. And then I wondered what to do. Billy said they would sail on the 21st and reach New York on the 29th, so I decided to go back to Rose Hill and begin to pack.

Father could not come to me, so I would go to Father and be home by the time Billy got there. It was only the 3d of September, but I decided I would leave as soon as I could do so without remarks being made about my going sooner than I expected, and to prevent remarks I would have to invent a good reason for getting away. Father's loneliness would make a perfect reason for Twickenham Town, and a most dutiful one, and no one would be apt to ask me why I hadn't thought of his loneliness before; but it wouldn't do for the family. They wanted me to stay out of the city as long as possible, and while I was wondering what I could do to get back, Mrs. Pettigrew passed with five of the children in the buggy and asked if I knew there was a telegram for me at the station. I told her I did not, and my heart got right where hearts always get when telegrams are mentioned, and in the twinkling of an eye Skylark's bridle was on and I on Skylark, and we raced like mad to town.

On the way I was thinking all the awful things that telegrams start one to thinking, and I remembered it was just eleven days since I had sent the letter to Billy, who had, of course, gotten it by this time, and, not realizing how fast I was going, I was at the station before it seemed possible to get there, and so out of breath I could not speak. I slipped off the horse and held out my hand to Mr. Pepper for the telegram, and when he handed me the yellow envelope I slid down on a bench and held it as if it were a death-warrant, and not for some time could I open it. I was positive it was about Mother, who wasn't very well when she last wrote, and everything I had ever done that I ought not to have done, and everything I had left undone which I should have done, walked right up in front of me and clutched me by the throat, and I had to shut my eyes to keep my head steady. I had inside the same sinky feeling I felt the first time I went to Europe, on the first day out.

Mr. Pepper was looking at me, and so were several other people who happened to be standing around, so I tried to get a grip on, and after awhile I opened the envelope; but at first I couldn't see the words on it. Finally I took them in after three times reading them over, and at last I understood.

Cut it out. You are engaged to me. Sailing to-morrow. See you September fifteenth. — BILLY.

CHAPTER XXVIII

There never was a sinner saved by grace who so wanted to make a noise as I wanted to make one when I got into my head what had happened. The relief from fear and the joyfulness of knowing I had been pulled out of another ditch made me dizzy for a moment, and down went my elbows into my lap and down my face into my hands, and not until Mr. Pepper said something to me did I lift my head and get up. Then I threw my riding-crop in the air, tossed up the Pepper baby, danced around with him, and, suddenly seeing all present were watching me, and knowing they felt they had a right to hear what was in the telegram without waiting for Mr. Pepper to tell them, I said an old friend of mine, who was anxious to know Twickenham Town, was coming to see it when he got back from Europe. After which I gave Mr. Pepper a little wink which he understood, and I am sure no one was told the wording of the message I had received. Mr. Pepper has a good deal of sense.

Happy? I was the happiest girl in all the world that day. I nearly sang my throat off when I got to my room, but I did not mention the telegram to anybody save Miss Susanna, and I didn't go into details with her about it. I just said a friend was coming to see me when he got back from Europe, and I said it in such a way she didn't think I was interested very much. She is so astonished by Elizabeth's behavior, and so surprised at her marriage, which is to be in November, that I don't think she paid any attention to what I said and got the impression it was a friend of Father's who was coming to Twickenham Town. I let her keep it. I did not give it to her knowingly, but there was no need to take it away.

And last night, not being able to sleep, I knew I had not been in love with Whythe at all. I don't know a thing in the world about being in love. I had tried to think I knew something, but I was mistaken. I must say I enjoyed hearing Whythe's crescendo, obligato, diminuendo way of making it, but I realize now I am not the sort of person to really fall in love with strange men. Certainly I could never do it with a wabbly, changery, one-or-the-othery kind of man that Whythe is, and while it was pretty scrumptious thinking a twenty-five-year-older was in love with me, I soon found out it was a summer case and not at all serious. And I am thankful I never thought I was enough in love to become engaged. There might have been things to remember that one likes to forget when the real one comes along, and I have nothing of that sort to be sorry for. I'm right particular at times.

If I am ever really and truly engaged I wonder if I will be as particular as a sixteen-year-old person, a girl person, ought to be? I guess it will depend on whom I am engaged to, but, of course, not being in love, I couldn't be engaged, and there is no use in thinking what I might do under circumstances that might warrant the doing of it, and when I see Billy I will just shake hands; that is—

Every time I think of his coming I feel like opening my arms so wide I could take the whole world in, but I don't open them. I just go look at the calendar to see if another day hasn't gone by yet. When this morning I saw it was the 14th and realized there wasn't but one more day to wait, I went to the window and did open my arms, and I sent a message into the air. And then, because I felt so sorry for Miss Araminta Armstrong, who has nothing to wait for but older age, and for Miss Bettie Simcoe, who has long since stopped hoping, I went down-stairs and asked them if they wouldn't like to motor to Glade Springs, and they said they would, and we went. Also Mr. Willie Prince. I didn't want to ask him, but I couldn't leave him out, and of course he wanted to go. The going made the day pass a little quicker, but it has been a long day! Awful long!

For the last week I have been going around to almost every house in town to say good-by. I don't know the exact day I will leave, as that will depend on when Mother says I must be home; but I didn't want to go away and not say good-by to everybody and tell them what a good time I have had, and I started telling very soon after I got Billy's message saying he was coming. I have thanked everybody for their niceness and kindness to me, and told every one I hope to come back next summer, and sometimes we have had little weeps, for they put their arms around me and held me so tight I could hardly breathe. And I know now there is nothing as good as friendliness, and loving-kindness is more to be desired than all things else on earth, and I am going to try to make it grow wherever I live. I will have a garden of it—have it in my heart.

I am afraid I will always have some practical things in my heart, too, for of late I've been thinking about all that money Billy had to spend in cabling me from Europe. When Billy wants to do a thing he never lets obstacles stand in his way, and he would have sent that cable if he'd had to borrow the money from the Bank of England at an awful rate of interest. What he did do I guess was to get it from his mother. She would take her head off and her heart out and hand both over if he wanted them, and it isn't her fault that William, as she calls him, isn't a ruined person.

I know she hated him to leave ahead of time, which he had to do to get here on the 15th, the rest not sailing, Jess says, until the 20th; but that's William again. He doesn't waste time when he has anything to attend to, and I know exactly what he said to his mother. He will make every arrangement and fix everything for them and then tell them good-by. He isn't much with words, Billy isn't. He acts. There's no fumble in him, and even his mother, who thinks his mold was broken when he was born and that the Lord never made but one like him, has to admit he is a high-handed person when occasion requires. I don't agree with his mother in a good many things concerning William, but in some I do. I wish he wasn't an only son. An only son for a husband is hard on a wife.

The thing I have been thinking about most since I got his cable, however, is a certain thing that was in it. I've worn the paper out reading it, and at first there was no argument in my mind, but it is coming, argument is. And though I know it is a bad habit, especially in girls and women and disliked by the other sex, how can you help it when things are said that are not so? Billy said, "You are engaged to me." How does he know? I never told him so. He hasn't exactly asked me—that is, in a way that I would answer him—and he always got so choky when on such subjects that I changed them quick, and yet he announces that I am his, and with never so much as by your leave!

I am afraid, I'm terribly afraid, I am going to agree with him. It's a relief to have some things settled for you, and as he imagines I will always be falling overboard, he doubtless thinks he had better keep a life-preserver on me in case he isn't near enough to jump in after me. He knows if I ever agree to put one on I will keep it on. I have a good deal of Father in me, and when I give my word I stick to it.

If any one had told me when I came to Twickenham Town that the chief thing I would find out before I went away was that I wouldn't really mind owning a life-preserver, my head would have gone up and I would have been as chesty as a hen who tries to crow; and now I'm nothing but a humble-minded person waiting for a high-handed one to come and take me back home. And I am perfectly willing to go. Another thing I have found out this summer is that it doesn't much matter where you are or what you are doing; whether there is purple and fine linen or just ancestors, or both together, or neither; if the one you want most isn't with you, you will be pretty lonely after a while.

I have had a grand time in Twickenham Town, but I don't want to come here again by myself. If Mrs. William Spencer Sloane wants to take her son away with her next summer, she won't be able to do it. Her son will be twenty-one next summer, and though I hope he will always be respectful and obedient, as far as possible, to his mother's wishes, still, she will have to remember there are other wishes in this world besides hers. I trust she will be nice about the discovery. Mrs. Sloane is a very handsome woman, but spoiled. And very fond of having her own way.

We are not apt to have much money, Billy and I. We have often said we thought young people ought to do their own scrambling, and I think that's what we'll have to do, as our fathers think much the same way. I'm not fond of herbs, but I can stand a dinner of them if Billy can, and besides, it will be nice for us to work up together and not have too quick a shove. And another thing we agree about. We know the thing that counts most, and we are going to keep a good deal of it on hand. Father says neither poverty nor riches can kill love if it is the right sort. I know Billy's is the right sort, but I am crazy to hear him put it into words.

He will have traveled thousands of miles to say something he could have written, to tell me I am engaged to him and I might as well understand it; but there won't be an extra sentence in the way he says it. He will be here to-morrow, and I bet the best thing I've got that all he will say is: "Kitty Canary, we are going to decide right now on the day and the month and the year. I will wait until you get through college, as you say I've got to, but I won't wait a day longer. Let's get a calendar and work it out."

And I, being a weak-minded person at times, will say, "All right, Billy," and then—

THE END